BRONCOS

and

BALLADS

Books by Jody Hedlund

Healing Springs Ranch
Spurs and Sparks
Broncos and Ballads

High Country Ranch
Waiting for the Rancher
Willing to Wed the Rancher
A Wife for the Rancher
Wrangling the Wandering Rancher
Wishing for the Rancher's Love

Colorado Cowgirls
Committing to the Cowgirl
Cherishing the Cowgirl
Convincing the Cowgirl
Captivated by the Cowgirl
Claiming the Cowgirl: A Novella

Colorado Cowboys
A Cowboy for Keeps
The Heart of a Cowboy
To Tame a Cowboy
Falling for the Cowgirl
The Last Chance Cowboy

A Shanahan Match
Calling on the Matchmaker

Saved by the Matchmaker

A Wager with the Matchmaker

Bride Ships: New Voyages

Finally His Bride

His Treasured Bride

His Perfect Bride

His Unforgettable Bride

Bride Ships Series

A Reluctant Bride

The Runaway Bride

A Bride of Convenience

Almost a Bride

Orphan Train Series

An Awakened Heart: A Novella

With You Always

Together Forever

Searching for You

Beacons of Hope Series

Out of the Storm: A Novella

Love Unexpected

Hearts Made Whole

Undaunted Hope

Forever Safe

Never Forget

Hearts of Faith Collection
The Preacher's Bride
The Doctor's Lady
Rebellious Heart

Michigan Brides Collection
Unending Devotion
A Noble Groom
Captured by Love

Historical
Luther and Katharina
Newton & Polly

Knights of Brethren Series
Enamored
Entwined
Ensnared
Enriched
Enflamed
Entrusted

Fairest Maidens Series
Beholden
Beguiled
Besotted

Lost Princesses Series
Always: Prequel Novella

Evermore

Foremost

Hereafter

Noble Knights Series
The Vow: Prequel Novella
An Uncertain Choice
A Daring Sacrifice
For Love & Honor
A Loyal Heart
A Worthy Rebel

Waters of Time Series
Come Back to Me
Never Leave Me
Stay With Me
Wait for Me

A HEALING SPRINGS RANCH NOVEL

BRONCOS
and
BALLADS

JODY HEDLUND

NORTHERN LIGHTS PRESS

Broncos and Ballads
Northern Lights Press
© 2025 by Jody Hedlund
Jody Hedlund Print Edition
ISBN 979-8-9896277-6-9

Jody Hedlund www.jodyhedlund.com

This is a work of fiction. All characters are products of the author's imagination. Any resemblance to actual events or locales or persons, living or dead, is entirely coincidental.

Cover Design by RoseannaWhiteDesigns.com

1

"'Is Brock McQuaid a fraud?'" Harper read the article heading on his tablet. "'He sings about love, but he's never been in love.'"

"I can admit I've never been in love." Brock sat on the seat of the Range Rover beside his manager. "But that doesn't make me a fraud."

At least, he hoped not.

Brock's gaze snagged on an enormous billboard off to the side of the Los Angeles highway leading away from the airport, where he'd landed a short while ago in his private jet. The billboard was of him—deep-brown eyes, square jawline with a permanent layer of scruff, wavy dark-brown hair beneath a cowboy hat, and his trademark crooked grin. His flannel shirt was unbuttoned, revealing one of his tattoos and his muscular chest. And he was holding his guitar with his sleeves rolled up, showing more tattoos on his forearms.

He'd almost grown immune to seeing himself like that, so much larger than life. The billboard was an advertisement for his world tour, which would conclude near the end of August in about a month—a month too long, if he was honest.

Harper scrolled to the next article. "'Ainsley Rose breaks the silence about her breakup with country music star Brock McQuaid.'"

"*Her* breakup?" Brock scoffed. "I'm the one who ended things." He'd done so last week and hadn't heard from Ainsley since. He'd hoped that meant she wasn't too hurt. But her scathing post about him yesterday on Instagram had dashed that hope. She'd obviously been more upset than she'd initially let on. Now every news outlet in the country had decided to report on what a terrible boyfriend he'd been.

His manager glanced up from his tablet, his gaze serious behind his glasses, the crinkles at the corners of his eyes more pronounced than usual. "It doesn't matter what actually happened, Brock. The point is, she'll tank your ratings, which have already started sliding into the toilet lately."

"Aw, c'mon. That's a little harsh."

"That's what you love about me. I never sugarcoat anything."

For once, Brock half wished Harper weren't so direct. But that's why Brock paid him the big bucks to be his manager. Because he was good at his job. In his usual dark-blue suit with a starched white dress shirt, Harper was as classy as always, his silvery-black hair clipped short around his bald crown, his beard trimmed neatly, and his accessories—watch, cuff links, and rings—expensive but not gaudy.

"'Lost in love?'" Harper read. "'McQuaid isn't lost *in* love. He's lost *about* love. He clearly has no idea what being in love is all about.'"

"Lost in Love" was the title of one of Brock's hit songs. Of course the tabloids would play on the words.

"That's not true," said Ella Mae from the front seat next to the chauffeur. Brock's twenty-something assistant tossed him a sympathetic glance. "Brock has plenty of women who will testify about his sweet lovin'."

Brock offered Ella Mae a grateful nod. With her long brown hair pulled up in a high ponytail and her face devoid of makeup, Ella Mae had a natural aura that made her less intense than Harper, which Brock appreciated, especially at times like this.

"'Brock McQuaid is falling fast and failing fast at love.'" Harper's voice was clipped in obvious irritation.

It appeared the media was having fun with their criticism. "Falling Fast" was the name of another top song.

At the ping of an incoming text, Harper turned to his phone, read the message, then frowned. "It's Steve, and he's livid at all the bad publicity."

"Surprise, surprise." Brock couldn't keep from being sarcastic.

Steve was always livid, and Brock put up with the label executive because, overall, he'd liked working with BMN—Blue Mountain Nashville. As one of the largest country music labels, they'd been a good home for him for the past seven years. Had helped launch him from obscurity into one of America's hottest stars, turning him into a household name so that now everyone in the world knew about him, even if they weren't a country music fan.

"He's flying out here today." Harper was reading the next text. "He wants to meet with us in order to come up with a damage-control plan."

"Brock doesn't have any free time." Ella Mae consulted the old-fashioned Day Timer she used to keep track of every minute of every day of Brock's life. He couldn't chew a piece of gum without having it penciled in.

"We need to make time." Harper was typing a text—probably one to Steve confirming a meeting.

"Brock has interviews all afternoon until Reed's party starts."

"Cancel them."

Ella Mae was still bent over the schedule. "Can't. Do you know how hard it was to get *L.A. Style* to fit him in today? And it took weeks to get the *Entertainment Tonight* spot."

Brock didn't mind the interviews. He liked talking with people and usually had no trouble just being himself. "Tell Steve I'll stop over in Nashville on my way back to Europe." He had a concert in Oslo, Norway, in a few days and from there was headed to Stockholm. But he could make the time to stop in Nashville before leaving, and while he was there, he could stay a night at the ranch he'd purchased last year. Maybe doing so would give him the boost he needed to finish the tour strong.

"Steve wants to meet today." Harper's tone said it was already a done deal. Ella Mae opened her mouth to protest again, but Harper cut her off. "We don't want Brock interacting with any press until we get a plan of action in place."

Ella Mae nodded. "We can let the reporters know the topic of Ainsley Rose is off-limits."

Brock was used to people talking about him in the third person as if he weren't in the room—or in this case the SUV. He was also used to his team making decisions for him. But sometimes all the talking made him feel like a child who couldn't think for himself instead of a twenty-nine-year-old adult. And sometimes he wished he could take back a little control of his life.

But the truth was, he had very little control. He'd learned from the start that if he wanted to be a star, he had to trust the people in the industry to use their expertise to make the stardom happen. They had, and now he had to trust them again to get him out of his current predicament.

"Brock can lie low for a few hours." Harper sent a text and then began reading another. "Reed did say that there won't be any press or paparazzi at the resort, right?"

Ella Mae flipped through her notes, then ran her finger down a list of items, probably related to the party. "Only the photographer he hired for the evening."

Reed Sawyer was another country music singer Brock had met early in his career. They'd both been signed on at about the same time by different labels. They'd performed at many of the same venues, had done similar opening acts, and had mingled at parties.

Reed had risen to stardom too—though maybe not quite as high or bright as Brock. But he was a good guy and had become a good friend. When he'd called and personally invited Brock to a party in Bel Air at a posh resort, Brock hadn't been able to turn him down, especially because Reed had sounded excited.

Brock suspected his friend was throwing the party in order to propose to his new girlfriend, Lexi King. He didn't know for certain if that's what was happening tonight, but Reed had been insistent that Brock be at the party, that he couldn't miss it.

Thankfully, Ella Mae had squeezed the visit into his

schedule after a few days in Colorado at his family's ranch for his dad's birthday. Everyone on his team had agreed Reed's party would give him the opportunity to make connections with Los Angeles media, which was something he didn't do often enough.

Now, with Ainsley Rose's critical Instagram post casting him in such a negative light, he would have to figure out a way to repair his image and make his fans remember why they loved him.

"Think you can lie low for the afternoon, Brock?" Harper glanced at him, his eyes keen behind his glasses. It wasn't so much of a question as it was a command.

Brock gave his manager a thumbs-up. "Course I can."

Brock lasted only an hour in his suite at the San Vicente Inn before going stir-crazy. With Harper and Ella Mae both busy, he put on his baseball cap and sunglasses, the usual disguise for going out when he didn't want to be recognized. The cover rarely worked. Maybe he was too recognizable. Or maybe so many celebrities used the hat-and-glasses disguise that it was no longer effective. Besides, all it took was one person to shout out his name for everyone to realize who he was.

He honestly didn't care if people recognized him and came up to him. He never minded talking to fans. But he had promised Harper he'd lie low, and so exploring incognito was his best option.

The place was stunning. Obviously it couldn't compare with Healing Springs Ranch, his family's upscale resort in Colorado, but it was still luxurious with a beautiful pool, a private golf course, expansive gardens, a large spa, a rooftop lounge, and a five-star restaurant.

As he climbed the stairs to reach the lounge, he paused and took in the view of the Santa Monica range with its jagged, rocky hillsides. It wasn't as stunning as the Rocky Mountains that had been his backyard while growing up. But it gave him a taste of home.

He pulled in a breath of fresh air before hiking the last few stairs. As he rounded to the spacious flat rooftop of the inn, he halted abruptly at the sight that greeted him. Directly ahead, a woman was climbing one of the trellises full of ivy and attempting to peer over the top at the lounge area on the other side.

She was wearing flat white sandals, a large white sun hat that concealed her hair, and a sheer white cover-up over a sleek pink bikini. From the elegance of the attire and the flashes of gold embellishment, she was clearly one of the resort's guests and not the gardener.

But why was she climbing the trellis? Was she attempting to spy on someone on the other side?

As she stretched higher, her hat lifted to reveal her face—one of the most beautiful faces in the world, one that graced the cover of countless magazines and billboards, one that made people everywhere turn their heads in admiration. High cheekbones, a slender nose, full lips, elegantly arched eyebrows, and a narrow chin. Wisps of her pale blond hair dangled by her ears.

Supermodel Venus Vargas.

Brock should have known she would be at the party. As Reed's best friend, she accompanied him to every big event—usually as his plus-one—stood beside him on the red carpet, sat next to him during awards ceremonies, and often vacationed with him.

Their relationship had puzzled Brock from the moment he'd met Venus at one of Reed's earliest concerts. He didn't understand how the two could remain platonic and never develop feelings for each other beyond friendship. But they had both claimed many times over the years that they were just friends and would never be anything more than that.

He wouldn't have been able to stay *just friends* with Venus. Nope. Whenever he was around her, the sparks of his attraction invariably flared to life. He was the kindling, and she was the flame. Getting too near and staying too long around her always had a way of making him feel too hot. As a result, he'd learned over the years to keep their interactions short and sweet and to admire her from afar.

She lifted her foot in the trellis and seemed to be

searching for another hold so that she could climb a little higher. In the same moment, her swimsuit cover snagged in a twig or branch or something, halting her upward climb.

With both of her hands grasping the top of the trellis, she tried to hoist herself and find another place for her foot, but the tangled swimsuit cover held her in place, not letting her budge.

She glanced down, released one hand, and tugged on the material.

It didn't move.

With only one hand and one foot now secure, she wobbled. It was only a matter of time before she fell.

With a surge of concern, Brock took several rapid steps toward her.

Upon hearing his footsteps, she shifted slightly, and her startled eyes landed upon him. The blue, as always, was clear and light and shimmery, like an iridescent mountain lake in the sunshine. Perfectly shaped and framed by long lashes, her eyes alone had the power to render a man speechless.

If only that was her best feature. But everything about her was incredible, including the body that was on display now that the swimsuit cover was slipping off. Her long legs were possibly her best feature. The slender but muscular legs were so enticing that he had no doubt she was the envy of every model and the dream of every man.

Of course, the rest of her body was just as gorgeous, and her pink swimsuit hugged every curve to perfection. But he forced himself not to linger over her body. She had enough men who lusted after her. He'd long ago told himself he wouldn't be one of them and would instead treat her the way Reed did, with respect.

She yanked more firmly at the tangled swimsuit cover, but the motion set her even more off-balance. Her foot within the trellis slipped, and in the next instant, she lost her grip on the top.

Brock could see the disaster unfolding. With nothing anchoring her to the trellis but her swimsuit cover, she toppled backward. He closed the gap between them just in time, holding out both arms.

"Oh no!" Her cry echoed in the silence along with a tearing sound as her cover-up stayed on the trellis while she tumbled into his arms. The bump against his shoulders and chest knocked her sun hat off her head, and her blond wavy hair spilled down from a loose knot.

Her arms reflexively wound around his neck.

Steadying himself, he drew her in closer, her back against one arm and her long legs dangling over the other. "Are you okay—"

Before he could finish the question, Venus clamped a hand over his mouth. Her elegant brows narrowed to a point, and she cast a glance in the direction of the lounge. "Shhh," she whispered.

With all the commotion she'd already caused with her fall, it was too late to worry about being quiet. In the next instant, sure enough, a young couple hurried around the trellis, their eyes wide.

Reed and Lexi.

Venus's expression went from grave to brightly happy so fast Brock nearly got whiplash.

At the sight of them, Reed halted abruptly. With sandy-blond hair, he was stockier than Brock, bigger boned, heftier in weight, and less fit. Reed was also shorter than Brock's six foot three by a couple of inches, but only a little taller than Venus, who had the long, slender body required of models.

At five feet ten inches, Venus had the perfect measurements of a model, including the perfect 34-24-34. Brock had read somewhere that the numbers stood for her bust, waist, and hips. Not that he'd looked for information on her. He just happened to stumble across it once in a while.

"Oh, hi, Reed." Venus turned her most charming smile upon her friend.

"Venus?" Reed's brows shot up. "Is everything all right?" His gaze landed upon the swimsuit cover now dangling from the trellis before turning back to Venus in her bikini.

"Everything is just fine." Her voice was too cheerful.

Again, Reed took her in, this time finally seeming to

notice Brock and the way he was holding Venus. "Hey, Brock. Nice to see you."

"Same with you, man."

Reed's gaze hopped back and forth between Brock and Venus, as though he was trying to solve the mystery of why the two of them were standing there like newlyweds about to walk off into the nearest bedroom. Just the merest thought of taking Venus into a bedroom made Brock's blood pump faster.

Lexi was watching them, too, with wide eyes, as though she hadn't expected to see them there together, especially in such an intimate hold. As a professional cheerleader for the Los Angeles Rams, Lexi was pretty in a perky way, with a voluptuous figure, thick fake eyelashes, and brown hair streaked with blond highlights.

Brock couldn't remember exactly how Reed had met Lexi earlier in the year—maybe at a party. She seemed sweet. And she was really into Reed.

An awkward silence descended over the terraced area. He supposed he and Venus should explain what they were doing and why her swimsuit cover was dangling in the ivy, but what *were* they doing? He still had no idea why Venus had come up to the lounge in the first place or why she'd been climbing the trellis.

"We were just..." Venus hesitated, as though she finally realized how strange their predicament looked. "Brock and I...we were just...um, having a private moment..."

Lexi's eyes lit up. With relief? "So you and Brock are a thing?" Was Lexi worried about Reed's relationship with Venus? If so, Brock didn't blame her. Not with the long history Reed and Venus had together and as close as they were.

"Are we a thing?" Venus's voice rose a note too high. Her gaze was upon Reed, practically begging him to walk across the terrace and intervene.

But Reed seemed to be waiting for an answer to Lexi's question.

Lexi sidled closer to Reed, intertwining her fingers with his possessively. Then she reached up her opposite hand and laid it across Reed's chest, tucking a couple of fingers through the space between the buttonholes of his dress shirt.

Brock had been around enough women to recognize what Lexi was doing. She was staking her claim on Reed.

Reed, however, just smiled at Venus, his expression as clueless as always at the dynamics playing out. "I know you like to keep relationships private," Reed said quietly. "But you know you can tell me—and Lexi—anything."

Brock hadn't heard much about Venus's dating life over the years of knowing her. Every once in a while, he'd seen a picture or two of her with a new guy. But most of the photos out there were of her with Reed.

Venus shifted in Brock's arms but didn't make a move to extricate herself. She was thin and light. Even if she hadn't been, Brock had a rigorous strength-and-conditioning routine every morning, and he could hold Venus all day. Not that he'd ever do that. Or that she'd let him. But still…

"Right, honey?" Reed slid his arm around Lexi.

"Yes, baby." She stood on her toes and kissed him…and kissed him. The lip-locking was showy and passionate with loud smooching sounds.

In Brock's arms, Venus stiffened more with each passing second.

Was Venus jealous?

"The truth is"—Venus lifted a hand to the back of Brock's head and combed at the strands that weren't concealed by his baseball cap—"Brock and I are exploring the possibility of a more serious relationship."

Reed broke the kiss to stare at Venus with disbelief.

"That's wonderful!" Lexi exclaimed, leaning into Reed. "Isn't it, baby?"

Venus peered up at Brock, her eyes shining with adoration—or at least the pretend variety.

Because that's what Venus was doing. She was pretending to like him. Why? To cover over the awkward situation she found herself in?

As she met his gaze, her eyes pleaded with him not to contradict her and to go along with her charade.

Venus Vargas was digging herself into a deeper hole by the second, but now that she was in it, she didn't know how to climb out.

The trouble was, she was dragging Brock McQuaid down into the hole with her.

His eyes, full of questions, held hers.

She'd been around Brock enough over the years to guess that he'd go along with her charade for now. He was fun-loving and easygoing and seemed to like challenges.

Hopefully he wouldn't call her out as a liar right here. Not in front of Lexi. Would he wait and let her talk with Reed in private first?

As though he'd heard her unspoken request, he nodded.

She gave a tiny nod back. Somehow she'd find a way to make this up to him, to thank him for saving her from utter humiliation.

But first, she would need to let Reed know how she really felt…that she'd been in love with him for years and wanted to marry him.

Why couldn't he see that? Had she gotten so good at hiding her true feelings that he believed what they'd both told the press, that there would never be anything between them except friendship?

She stifled a sigh.

Why had she decided it was a good idea to spy on Reed and Lexi?

One of Lexi's hands was nearly stuffed into Reed's shirt, and the other was rubbing up and down his arm. And her lips were swollen from the kisses she'd just shared with Reed—kisses that didn't belong to her, kisses she'd obviously facilitated because she was jealous, kisses that Reed had no choice but to give back.

If only Lexi wasn't so pushy…

"I'm so happy for you and Brock." Lexi plastered on one of her gametime cheerleader smiles. "You're perfect for each other."

"Perfect for each other?" A new voice came from the other side of the trellis, and a moment later, a man stepped outside of the lounge into the waiting area. He was holding an expensive camera in one hand and a phone in his other. Lanky, with long blond hair pulled back into a ponytail, the man was Peter Flemming, a freelance photographer that many celebrities used for private affairs.

Had he just overheard the whole conversation about being in a relationship with Brock McQuaid?

The small bubble of panic from earlier swelled inside her. She hadn't meant to lie. It was just that with Lexi hanging onto Reed as if she wanted to gobble up every inch of him, the words had taken wing and escaped before she'd been able to cage them.

If only she hadn't overheard two of the staff at the pool talking about how Reed planned to propose to Lexi tonight during the party, that essentially the gathering was their engagement party.

Venus had panicked and fled from the pool, desperate to find Reed and have him reassure her that he wasn't getting engaged, that he wasn't ready to settle down yet, and that he was busy with his career. Because that was everything he'd been telling her for years.

For the most part, his inability to commit hadn't been a problem for Venus. She hadn't been ready to settle down either, had been equally as busy with her career.

She'd searched the resort on a mission to corner Reed and find out what was going on. Yes, she knew he liked Lexi. But she hadn't expected him to get so serious, had thought Lexi was another passing fling like previous women.

The truth was, she'd assumed she was Reed's girl, that

when he was ready to commit, he'd let their friendship blossom into more. She was ready for more. She'd been ready for a while. She'd just been patiently waiting for him.

When she'd located the couple in the rooftop lounge, she'd heard the happiness in Reed's laughter, and she'd needed to know more, needed to hear more. So she'd done the first thing that had come to her mind and climbed the trellis, hoping to eavesdrop and maybe even view them from above.

She might have done so if Brock McQuaid hadn't startled her.

"Yes, I do agree with you, Lexi," Peter was saying as he cocked his head and studied Venus in Brock's arms. "They do look perfect together. Almost as perfect as you and Reed."

With a hop of positive energy and another bright smile, Lexi pressed a kiss to Reed's lips again. But this time he was too busy staring to respond. His brows were pulled together into a stormy line, and his handsome hazel eyes were filled with concern.

Concern over what? Maybe seeing her with another man made him jealous.

"Actually, you two look stunning." Peter was still examining her. "Can I photograph the two of you together?"

"That's not a good idea," Reed replied.

"Okay. Why not?" Brock said at the same time.

With Brock holding her almost effortlessly, she lifted one of her arms and one of her legs into the carefree pose she'd perfected. She angled her head closer to Brock so that they looked more intimate, and she turned on her most flirty smile.

Peter had already ducked behind the lens of his camera and was shooting pictures rapidly. "Beautiful," he crooned.

"As beautiful as I am," Brock said in a playful tone, "I'm told I need to lie low and not make any waves on social media."

"No worries." Peter lowered his lens. "All the pictures from today and the party tonight are strictly for Reed and Lexi and no one else."

Reed's scowl remained firmly in place. "We won't need any pictures of Brock and Venus."

"Now, baby." Lexi's lips curved into a pout. "Be excited for them. They deserve to be just as happy as we are, don't they?"

"Of course." Reed caught Venus's gaze and seemed to be trying to see into her soul and find the truth. But she'd been hiding the truth about her feelings for so long that she'd gotten really good at keeping them out of sight.

She smiled at him, a dazzling smile that usually softened his irritation.

He tried to smile back, all the while avoiding looking

at Brock. "We need to talk."

"Sure." Relief rushed in to replace the panic from moments ago. Surely by seeing her in Brock's arms, Reed was already realizing what he was losing. They would talk, clear up the confusion, and then move forward with the relationship they were destined to have.

"I'll look for you later," he said, "before the party."

"I'll be waiting." She tried not to sound too eager, but from the pinch in Lexi's forehead, she guessed she hadn't succeeded.

As Reed walked back toward the lounge, Lexi slipped her arm around his waist and plastered herself to his side.

She was so handsy with him, always touching him. He had to find that overbearing. In fact, he had to find so many things about her over-the-top. Venus knew Reed and knew the type of woman he liked. And Lexi, with her outgoing and loud personality, was not who he needed for a life partner. He needed someone more serious, independent, and deep. Someone like her.

They'd already bonded as friends because of how similar their personalities and interests were. They came from the same background, from wealthy families in Malibu. They liked the same serious movies. They liked the same types of organic and healthy food. They liked the same upscale vacations. They could talk about anything, although lately Reed had been calling less often and the conversations had been shorter. She'd thought it was because they'd been working in opposite time zones and had kept crazy work hours.

She considered Reed her best friend, and she'd always told him that any girlfriend would have to accept her as his best friend, too, or that woman wouldn't be right for him. Of course, Venus had never imagined he would actually choose someone besides her.

When only she and Brock remained in the waiting area of the lounge, she released an exasperated sigh.

"I don't mind holding you." Brock's voice was lighthearted. "I might even hold my *girlfriend* the rest of the day."

What had she just done? She mentally slapped herself before wiggling and freeing herself from his grasp. As he placed her down gently to her feet, she took a rapid step away from him.

His gaze slid over her bikini-clad body before shifting to the mountain range that spread out to one side of the resort.

She was accustomed to men staring at her in all kinds of clothing, some even as revealing as a bikini. She was used to her body being handled and poked and prodded and repositioned and moved around. It was her job, she'd grown a thick skin, and she rarely took offense or took anything too personally.

But at Brock's effort not to stare at her body, she wasn't quite sure what to think, and she felt oddly bare.

She stepped toward the trellis and yanked on her swimsuit cover. It didn't come loose now any more than it had earlier.

Before she could voice her frustration, Brock was beside her and tugging on the garment. In the next instant, it came loose, leaving only a small sliver of the sheer material behind. He also swiped up her hat. Without glancing her way, he held out the items.

"Thank you." She quickly put both back on. "Can we discuss things?"

He was peering at the mountain range. "Might be a good idea—"

"But not here." Not where Reed or Lexi or Peter could overhear their conversation.

She headed down the stairs to the lobby. At midafternoon, the area was deserted, with only the staff at the front desk and a valet.

Even so, she crossed to a side room with tall potted trees surrounding a cluster of plush chairs and couches. She wanted to rush off and leave Brock and the embarrassment of the incident behind. But she waited for him to catch up.

He sauntered down the last flight of stairs. She'd been too busy on the rooftop to pay him attention. But now without any distractions, she took him in—attired in his usual jeans, cowboy boots, and formfitting T-shirt that showed off his well-defined muscles. Although the sunglasses were off, he was still wearing a baseball cap but had situated it backward.

Heartthrob. She'd heard that word used to describe Brock McQuaid. And it was true. With his dark hair and eyes, his chiseled face, his brawny build, and his boy-next-door charm, he was easily America's most eligible bachelor.

Even if a person didn't like country music—which she'd learned to like to support Reed—Brock had a rugged, gritty singing voice that drew fans in droves. She could admit a few of Brock's songs were on her favorites playlist. Okay, maybe more than a few.

There wasn't anything about Brock she disliked. He'd always been friendly and sweet and kind to her whenever they'd crossed paths. He'd also been a steady friend for Reed, which was hard to come by in such a competitive industry, where many musicians climbed over each other to reach the top.

As Brock headed toward her, he had a relaxed air about him, like he didn't have a care in the world. She knew that wasn't true. He'd had a slew of criticism yesterday and today about his breakup with Ainsley Rose. Venus hadn't heard much about the parting of ways, since she'd been in Rome for a fashion show until last night. But apparently Ainsley Rose had posted something negative on social media about Brock, and now fans were lashing out at him.

Venus had never liked Ainsley Rose. As a pop singer, the young woman had a decent following with a couple of hits in the past year or two. But on a personal level, Ainsley Rose was a diva, and Brock had been a saint to put up her with her for as long as he had.

Brock entered the sitting room, crossed to one of the sofas, then plopped down. He stretched out his long legs, crossing them at the ankles. Then he extended both arms along the back of the sofa, seeming completely at ease with her.

Not many people could be around her and feel comfortable. They were usually overwhelmed by her supermodel status, her appearance, or her intense aura. She'd been described as intimidating, serious, fierce, strong, and even cold at times. It was her image—what people expected when they saw her on the runway, on covers, and in ads.

Yes, she could admit she wasn't a bubbly person. But underneath it all, she liked to think she had a softer side. Maybe it didn't come out often, but it was still there.

"So…" Brock drummed his fingers on the back of the sofa.

She lowered herself to the chair across from him, perching on the edge. "I regret that I had to involve you in my drama, but if you hadn't startled me, I wouldn't have fallen—"

"Whoa now, darlin'." His brown eyes were a

mesmerizing shade of rich dark sable. "Even if I hadn't come along, you would've fallen. There's no way that trellis would have held you much longer."

"Perhaps." She loved his soothing accent. It wasn't Southern, but it had a twang of country to it and suited him. "Regardless, I ended up in your arms, and it seemed only logical for Reed and Lexi to assume we were a couple."

Brock's famous crooked grin kicked up. "Yep, it was only logical since you actually told them we were considering *the possibility of a more serious relationship.*"

She frowned. She supposed she had led everyone to believe more existed between her and Brock. "Very well, I accept full responsibility for misleading them."

Brock tapped the sofa again, shifting his gaze to the large picture window that overlooked the manicured gardens behind the inn. His grin faded, and his expression turned pensive.

"Listen," she started. "I'm sorry for creating a sticky situation for you. But once I have the chance to talk to Reed—"

"He's not going to give up Lexi for you." Brock's gaze swung back to her.

"I'm not expecting him to."

"Yep, you are."

That was what she was hoping for, wasn't it? For

Reed to give up Lexi and choose her instead. She'd be lying to deny it.

"I always thought that your whole 'friend thing'"—Brock used air quotes around the words—"couldn't be true, and I was right."

She stood abruptly, fisted her hands on her hips, and glared down at Brock. "It is true."

"It's obvious you want more than friendship with Reed."

Was it obvious? With the news of the possible engagement, had her carefully crafted walls cracked, allowing her real feelings to show?

It was her turn to stare out the window. She didn't see anything because her head was filled with images of the way Reed and Lexi had kissed, as if they truly did love each other. But how was that possible?

Venus gave a curt shake of her head. Reed was supposed to fall in love with her. They were supposed to have a classic case of friendship to more, best friends to lovers.

Brock spoke again, his voice gentle. "I'm guessing Reed doesn't know you care about him as more than friends?"

She shrugged one shoulder. She wanted to deny Brock's conclusion, but what was the point? "I heard the staff saying that Reed is planning to propose to Lexi tonight."

"So you were trying to listen in on their conversation to find out if it's true?"

"Yes, and then after I fell and they came running, I didn't want them to know I was there eavesdropping. I panicked and didn't know how else to explain my presence except that I was with you."

"Have you considered having an actual honest conversation with Reed about how you feel?"

She'd kept her feelings from Reed for so long that dumping them on him wouldn't be fair. "I don't want to ambush him."

Brock's brow quirked. "Ambush is better than deception, don't you think?"

Was it? A part of her had always been afraid that if she was too honest with Reed, he'd push her away. Then not only would she lose him as the love of her life, but she'd also lose her best friend, and she wasn't willing to make that kind of sacrifice.

"I'm planning to talk to him later." She started to cross toward the door, needing plenty of time to get ready for that meeting. She had to be stunning so that she could wow Reed and finally get him to take notice of her as a woman and not just a friend. "I'll do my best to clarify the situation and get you out of it."

She made it to the door before Brock spoke. "Don't worry about me, darlin'. You just take care of yourself."

She paused. None of this was his doing, and she

couldn't take her petty feelings out on him. Drawing in a steadying breath, she straightened her shoulders. "Thank you, Brock. You're a nice guy."

With that, she exited the room, leaving America's heartthrob behind for some other woman to have—in pretense or otherwise.

3

"Brock needs to fall in love." Steve's clipped, businesslike tone contained a finality that rubbed Brock the wrong way.

Truthfully, there was so much about Steve that rubbed Brock the wrong way that lately he'd begun to consider if Blue Mountain Nashville was really the right label for him. They'd been home to him and his albums since the start of his career, but there were times—like now—when he still felt like the twenty-two-year-old college graduate instead of an almost-thirty-year-old.

"I agree." Harper was sorting through the newspaper articles Steve's assistant had printed, which were now scattered on the conference room table in front of them. "If Brock falls in love, he'll be able to tell his fans he broke up with Ainsley Rose because he was waiting for the right woman."

Steve clicked his pen on then off, one of his habits

when he was nervous. "That will squelch all her rumors about how Brock is afraid of commitment."

In his mid-thirties, Steve was a fairly young man for an executive and had a lot of pressure to prove himself to the label.

Brock was sympathetic to feeling pressure. He'd experienced his share too. But lately, Steve had stooped to using unethical, even underhanded, tactics to get things done, and Brock wasn't a fan of working that way.

Brock glanced at his watch. Only an hour until the party started. They needed to wrap up the meeting so he could get ready. But since Steve and his assistant had made the trip from Nashville all the way to Bel Air specifically to do damage control of Brock's image, Brock had been patient and had tried to cooperate as they'd tossed around the options.

"I still think ignoring Ainsley Rose is for the best." Brock leaned back in the leather rolling chair. "Her bitter posts will blow over and be yesterday's news in no time."

"As I said"—Steve clicked his pen faster—"Ainsley Rose isn't your only problem. There are other previous girlfriends coming forward and saying the same thing."

The backlash was only growing worse as the day went on—that Brock McQuaid couldn't commit, didn't know what true love was, wasn't capable of loving, was only out to have a good time, and didn't believe anything he sang about in his songs.

"You need to fall in love, Brock." Steve spoke as if the matter were settled. "Go on out and get the job done."

Brock held back an irritated sigh. "Falling in love isn't that simple." He should know. He'd been trying for years to find the kind of love his dad had with his mom. The McQuaid legacy of love—the kind of love that generations of McQuaid men had developed for just one special woman, the kind that happened fast and furious and was strong and passionate and forever.

Brock had written about that kind of love in some of his early songs, using his dad as inspiration. And he'd hoped for the McQuaid legacy to happen to him so that he could experience the intensity of such a love.

But with each passing year, he'd begun to think he'd be an exception to the legacy, that maybe he'd never find a special woman who would change the trajectory of his life like it had changed the McQuaid men who'd come before him.

He'd drawn some solace over the past summer when his older brother, Ty, had found the woman of his dreams. If Ty could find his special woman after a bad marriage and being a single dad, then maybe Brock still could too.

But after years of already trying to fall in love, he couldn't do it on a whim or by force. It was too big of a decision, and he didn't want to choose the wrong woman.

"I know someone who specializes in setting up

couples," Steve was saying. "We'll contact her, have her sign a nondisclosure, then you can meet with her and tell her the kind of woman you want."

"Aw, c'mon." Brock just shook his head, fighting a rising swell of frustration. "I don't need someone finding me a woman."

"It's not as bad as it sounds. She's sort of like a living dating app. She'll narrow down the choices based on your preferences, and then she'll arrange for you to go out on a few dates. That's all."

Steve exchanged a glance with his assistant, who nodded and began to type on her laptop, probably composing an email to the relationships specialist.

"Hold on." Brock pushed back from the table. "Even if I find a woman I like, falling in love takes time."

"We don't have time. Not if we want to keep you from dropping any lower in the charts."

Brock shook his head. Before he could protest further, the door swung open, and Ella Mae poked her head in. Her brows were drawn. "We've got a new development."

Harper waved her inside. "What kind of development?"

"It's not good." Ella Mae stepped into the conference room and closed the door behind her even as she scrolled on her tablet.

Harper frowned, his glasses slipping down his nose. "Another past girlfriend airing her dirty laundry?"

In answer, Ella Mae flipped her tablet around to reveal a picture on Instagram, one of Brock in his ball cap and sunglasses, holding Venus Vargas in his arms. She was posing, like she had for the photographer on the rooftop, with a pretty smile, showing off her amazing legs and revealing a tantalizing amount of skin in her pink bikini.

She was drop-dead gorgeous, as always.

"We said no pictures." Steve frowned at the photo.

"I told them that." Brock couldn't tear his gaze from Venus and how stunning she was. "The photographer assured me he wouldn't post any." Not in those exact words, but close.

Ella Mae pointed to the top of the picture and the name listed. "Lexi posted it."

"I told Lexi I had to lie low."

"Well, it's out there, along with her congratulations to both you and Venus for being a happy couple in love. She posted it an hour ago, and it already has fifty thousand likes and hundreds of comments."

Brock had assumed Lexi knew *lying low* meant no pictures on social media. But apparently she didn't understand how things worked in the industry. "Great. What do we do now?"

"What's the reaction?" Steve asked, punching buttons on his phone, likely trying to reach the account. "Good or bad comments?"

"A mix." Harper was already on the post, reading the comments. "Some are saying Brock broke up with Ainsley Rose to date Venus, that he was cheating on Ainsley Rose, and that he's a scumbag. But others say they're excited Brock has finally found love, that they make a beautiful couple, and that Venus is better than Ainsley Rose."

The room grew silent, with only the laughter from passing guests filtering in. Harper, Steve, and Ella Mae continued to read the comments. But Brock didn't bother going to his account. He rarely looked at social media since it was so overwhelming. He had a publicist at the label who took care of all his social media posts. All Brock had to do once in a while was send over requested photos.

"Listen." Brock stood and pushed in his chair. "I'll talk to Venus, warn her about the post, and we'll release a statement together letting everyone know we're only friends."

Harper tossed Brock a raised-brow look. "Why exactly did Lexi lie about you and Venus? You guys could sue her for libel. She should know that."

Brock rubbed at the back of his neck, feeling sudden tension there. He didn't want to reveal the exchange he'd had with Venus about Reed. But he had to say something to defend Lexi.

"Well?" Steve joined the grilling. "What happened?"

"Venus and I...I was exploring the resort and ran into her."

"And…" Steve persisted.

Shoot. Brock didn't know how to spin the story. He didn't want to outright lie, but telling Harper and Steve and Ella Mae the truth about Venus trying to make Reed jealous wasn't an option. "We decided to have a little fun fooling people. That's all."

"That's all?" The sarcasm in Harper's tone said he hadn't bought the tale.

"It's not all. But it's all I can say without betraying Venus's trust in me."

Harper and Steve held gazes, as if they were both coming up with the same plan to make him spill the rest of the story.

Brock started toward the door. They'd gotten all they would from him. "I'm off to find Venus."

Ella Mae tucked her tablet into a bag hanging from her shoulder. "There's no time. You have to get dressed for the party."

"I need to warn Venus about Lexi's post first."

"No, no need to warn her." Steve stood, a slow smile that was more like a smirk making an appearance. "She's the solution to your problem."

With one hand on the doorknob, Brock halted. Whenever Steve gave that sly smile, Brock always knew he wouldn't like what the man was about to say.

"She's the new love of your life," Steve continued with too much confidence. "The woman you've been waiting for, the one you can't live without. You'll go out and make a statement tomorrow, letting the world know you and Ainsley Rose were separated for a while before the breakup."

That much was true. He and Ainsley Rose had been on the outs for the past month at least. She'd met up with him in Europe, and they'd spent a couple of days together. Near the end of their time, she'd pressured him about taking their relationship to the next level by making a deeper commitment to one another. She hadn't exactly said she wanted to get engaged, but he'd known that's what she'd been implying. When he'd told her he wasn't ready for engagement and marriage, she'd gotten angry and left.

They hadn't seen each other since and had stopped texting and calling. Finally, during his past week off between concerts, he'd visited Ainsley Rose before going home for his dad's birthday party, and he'd put an end to their relationship. He'd assumed she'd been in agreement about going their separate ways, but she'd obviously harbored more resentment than she'd let on.

Harper and Ella Mae didn't speak and were watching Steve, skepticism filling their eyes.

Steve continued on anyway. "You'll tell the press that Ainsley Rose made her claims about you being a fraud because she's jealous of your new relationship with Venus."

Brock shook his head. "That's not gonna happen. It's one thing to pretend something with Venus. But it's another thing entirely to drag down Ainsley Rose."

"She dragged you down first."

"It doesn't matter. I won't talk bad about her."

Steve pinned a narrowed gaze upon Brock. "What other choice do you have? How else are you going to explain Lexi's post?"

Brock scrambled to find another excuse he could give to the news outlets that would be clamoring to know about him and Venus and how it was related to Ainsley Rose—even though it wasn't related at all.

"We need to stay on top of this." Harper's tone held a warning. "You know that's why we're having this meeting today in the first place, right? Because we care about your career and want to keep you from suffering more backlash."

"I know." If they didn't provide answers, the rumors and speculation would only grow and harm him even worse. "But Venus will never go for that kind of plan."

Even though she'd tried to save herself from humiliation by claiming to be in a relationship with him, she was in love with Reed. It was one thing to fib to Reed and Lexi to save face in an embarrassing moment. It was another thing altogether to lie to the press and the world about being in a serious relationship, especially when the only man she wanted was Reed.

"I'll take care of it." Harper began to gather his notepad and pen and papers on the conference table. "We'll contact her agent and publicist and work something out."

Brock shrugged. "You can try. But don't be surprised if she says no."

"In the meantime, roll with it, play along with Venus."

He could only hope Venus had been able to talk to Reed. Maybe then he'd think twice about getting engaged to Lexi.

Brock should have guessed why Reed had organized the party and invited all his closest friends and family. But he hadn't taken Reed as the sort of guy who would rush into an engagement. Reed had always been cautious and careful when it came to women.

Maybe if Venus took the first step in sharing that she cared, Reed would reciprocate. Brock couldn't imagine how Reed wouldn't have feelings for Venus in return. How could any man not have feelings for her?

Regardless, Brock needed to find her as soon as possible so that he could tell her not only about Lexi's post—if she hadn't already seen it—but also about the publicity stunt his people were cooking up. He wanted her to know he'd had nothing to do with the idea and that he wished her all the best with Reed.

Venus felt every eye in the garden swing to her as she stepped outside under the sparkling lights strung over the arboretum.

She'd chosen the black silk Chanel mini dress she'd worn at a recent fashion show. The spaghetti straps revealed her elegant shoulders and neck, the short skirt showcased her legs, and the camellia lace at her waist gave a teasing show of skin too. She'd styled her hair into a sleek updo so that her long diamond earrings sparkled along her neck. Her makeup was painted on to perfection, including ruby red lipstick that added a pop of color to the otherwise dark outfit.

Tonight of all nights, she wanted to be stunning. To impress Reed.

She spotted him near the banquet tables under a white tent. He was sipping champagne and eating hors d'oeuvres with Lexi by his side, his attention focused on her. He looked incredible in a tan suit over a white shirt and a eucalyptus-green tie that matched Lexi's flowy gown of the same color. With his hair slicked back and his face tanned, his expressive features looked even more handsome than usual.

If only she'd had the chance to talk to him before the party had started. She'd texted him and invited him to her room. He'd said he'd come, but at the last minute claimed he didn't have time. So she'd resigned herself to singling him out at the party and asking for a moment alone.

Should she do so now?

The shadows had lengthened with the evening, and she tugged up the silky tulle draped over her shoulders as a sort of shawl. It was more for decoration than warmth, and with the cooler temperatures of the higher elevation, maybe she should have chosen a different outfit.

As she stepped away from the door, several of the closest guests greeted her, a curiosity in their eyes that was different from usual. She supposed it had something to do with Lexi's Instagram post from the afternoon, pairing her with Brock McQuaid. When her agent had texted her the picture, Venus had glanced only long enough to see that it was the picture Peter Flemming had taken of her in Brock's arms.

Even though her agent had also sent her the caption—something about congratulating the happy couple for their love—Venus had given little thought to the post. The media and paparazzi liked to make a big deal whenever she spent time with a man, conjecturing about whether she was finally dating someone. This time would be no different.

She'd later tell the press Lexi had been mistaken, that just because she and Brock had spent some time together didn't mean they were a couple. It would make Lexi look like a fool, but she shouldn't have posted something without asking.

Venus smiled and made small talk and mingled, slowly inching her way toward Reed. She only made it halfway before the resort door opened and Brock stepped out.

The attention shifted his way and conversations lulled. She didn't want to show any interest in Brock, knew ignoring him would squelch the rumors more quickly. However, her gaze was drawn to him anyway.

In his dark-gray three-piece suit, he looked more like a wealthy gentleman than a country singer. He wasn't wearing his usual cowboy hat or the ball cap from earlier, and his dark hair was combed neatly back with styling gel. His suit coat stretched taut over his shoulders and biceps, and his trousers were close-fitting, as was the current fashion. The five-o'clock shadow did nothing to hide the hard lines of his face—his strong, square jaw that flowed into equally strong, well-defined cheeks and a broad forehead.

There was no sense in denying it. Brock McQuaid was a hot specimen of manhood, one of the best-looking men she'd ever seen—and that was saying a lot, because she knew dozens of male models who were at the top of the scale of good looks.

Brock shoved his hands into his pockets, paused, and peered out over the crowd. He had an air of self-confidence that said he was used to people admiring him and wasn't bothered by it. After all, he stood on stages and sang and played his guitar in front of thousands of people on a regular basis. He could face a small group at a party like this and not even blink.

Several women immediately approached Brock, smiling in excitement and hoping to catch his attention. He nodded but sidled past them, his gaze sweeping over the crowd until halting on her. Those deep, dark eyes reached across the distance and yanked at something inside her. A strange tug.

Without breaking his gaze, Brock started toward her, each stride long and certain and unswerving. He didn't answer anyone, didn't even seem to notice the greetings and questions as he made his way directly to her.

When he stopped, she was oddly breathless, waiting for him to tell her she was beautiful or some other effusive compliment that men usually paid.

But instead of dropping his gaze to her dress, he held her eyes. Something there was serious, almost grave. "I need to talk with you privately for a moment."

She hesitated. She didn't have time for this. She needed to speak with Reed before he got down on one knee in front of Lexi. From the corner of her eye, Venus could see that he was finally looking at her after ignoring her since she'd joined the party.

Should she play up this interaction with Brock just a little? After all, Reed didn't know yet that the relationship was pretend. Maybe she could get another reaction out of him like she had outside the rooftop lounge.

He'd been upset at her for being with Brock. But why? Although she'd thought about it over the past few hours, she still didn't understand the reaction. She hoped it meant he didn't like her being with another man…because he cared about her and needed to admit it, although he wasn't usually upset at her when she went out on her infrequent dates.

Whatever the case, Venus could see a determination in Brock's stance that said he wouldn't be swayed from talking with her.

Pairing off alone would only cause more gossip about the two of them being a thing. But with a shrug, she stepped toward him, tucked her hand into his arm, and began to walk away from the gathering toward another area of the spacious garden with its maze of flowerbeds, shrubs, and water fountains.

As they headed down one of the flagstone paths, she

could feel the gazes following them. What must Reed think now? And was she hoping he would get jealous?

That was ridiculous. And immature of her.

Even so, as she turned a corner, she couldn't stop herself from casting a glance in his direction to find that he was still watching her with a furrowed brow and a frown.

He *was* jealous of Brock.

A small sense of satisfaction wafted through her. Maybe she didn't need to have a conversation with Reed after all. What if she just allowed him to go on thinking she and Brock were a couple for a while longer? She didn't have to resolve the misunderstanding tonight, did she? Tomorrow would come soon enough to let him know that she wasn't really with Brock.

But what about his proposal to Lexi? She didn't want him to get engaged, especially so publicly.

"We've got a problem." Brock surveyed the secluded nook as if making sure they were alone. No one else was in sight, and the trimmed shrubs provided a barrier between them and the other guests. A small pond with a bubbling fountain at the center was surrounded by several stone benches and exotic flowers in planters.

She released her hold on Brock's arm and walked to the edge of the pond. A moment later, she felt his presence beside her. He had a powerful, magnetic aura that was difficult to ignore.

"I'm sorry," he started.

She waved a hand. "If this is about Lexi's post, I'll straighten things out."

He was quiet for a beat. "Then my people haven't talked with yours yet?"

She shot him a sideways glance. His brown eyes were darker than usual, almost the color of a thick, soft corduroy. "Why would your people want to talk with mine?"

He cleared his throat and stuffed his hands back into his trouser pockets, pulling the material tighter. "They came up with a plan to deal with Lexi's post."

Venus's phone was in her clutch, which was tucked under one arm. All the while she'd been getting ready, her agent had been texting and calling. She'd finally sent a quick message back to Kristin that she couldn't talk and would call later. But mostly, she'd just ignored the texts and calls.

Was this what Kristin had wanted to discuss? Why she'd been calling nonstop for a while? Because of Brock?

Brock's shoulders slumped. "I just wanted to let you know I wasn't the one to come up with the plan, and I told them you wouldn't go through with it."

"Through with what?" She turned to face him.

He stared straight ahead. "Since my breakup with Ainsley Rose is causing some chaos, my manager thinks I need to prove that I know about love."

Everything was falling into place now. "So they're hoping I'll keep up a relationship to give you time to repair your image?"

"I told them no. That I didn't want to do it."

"Really?" She wasn't sure why his refusal surprised her, but it did.

"Really. And I didn't tell them anything about Reed."

"But they wanted to know why I started this?"

"I told them we were just fooling around and having a little fun."

"Did they buy it? Because most people know I don't fool around."

He shrugged. "Naw, they didn't really buy it. But they didn't pry any further."

Another beat of silence passed between them, and she shifted to look at the pond.

"Did you talk to Reed?" Brock's question was low.

She wished she didn't have to answer him, but he'd taken the time to warn her of the coming barrage from their managers. The least she could do was be honest back. "I didn't have the chance yet. I was making my way over to him."

"I hope it goes well."

"You hope what goes well?" The voice belonged to Reed and was laced with irritation. In the next instant, he stepped into the clearing behind them.

A sudden burst of panic raced through her. What

should she say to Reed? How could she ask him about the engagement without giving away her feelings? Or was it time to reveal them to him?

Brock straightened the lapels of his suit coat. "I'll leave you to it."

She wasn't sure if he was talking to her or Reed, but as he took a step away, she grabbed his arm.

He halted abruptly, glancing first at her hands clutching him, then lifting his dark eyes to hers. They were filled with compassion and kindness, something she didn't often see directed her way, particularly by a man.

"Do you want me to stay?" he whispered.

She'd always liked Brock for being such a decent guy. And he was proving himself to be more than decent. She was tempted to take up his offer, but she shook her head. "I'll be all right."

She forced herself to release his arm, but he held her gaze a moment longer, as though imparting strength to her. Then he walked away. As he passed by Reed, he nodded. Reed didn't nod back and instead glared.

Once Brock was out of sight, Reed crossed toward her, his brows still drawn. "You can't be serious about dating Brock."

She wasn't serious at all, but she didn't like Reed's condescending tone. "He's a great guy—"

"He's a player who can't make a serious commitment to any woman."

"I see you've been reading all the gossip about him and Ainsley Rose."

"It's hard to miss."

"You know you can't believe everything you hear."

"I'm friends with Brock, and it's more than hearsay. I've seen him in action, and I know how he is."

"I've seen Brock too. He might be a flirt, but he also has a really genuine side." She wasn't sure why she was defending Brock, except that he'd been so nice about everything today. And maybe she was just a little mad at Reed and couldn't hold back her frustration.

Reed's suit coat strained against his body but in a different way than Brock's had, probably because Reed was bigger and less fit. In her two-inch heels, she was as tall as him, if not taller. Even so, Reed Sawyer was a good-looking man. She'd always thought so, right from the moment they'd met in their senior year of high school.

"Brock is a good friend," Reed said. "But he's not boyfriend material for you."

Was this the jealousy speaking or concern in warning her away from a man that might have the potential to hurt her? Not that Brock could hurt her in a fake relationship. But still...

"What's the real issue here, Reed? Because you've never been opposed to anyone else I've dated."

"You haven't dated anyone else."

"Yes, I have."

"You've *gone out* on dates, but you haven't had a serious boyfriend."

He was right, and she suddenly hated that he was. Had she been waiting for him all this time?

She gave a shake of her head. Of course not. Not all those years. Maybe for part of them, over the past few years since she'd realized how much her feelings for him had grown. But before that she'd just been busy with her career and hadn't made time for a serious boyfriend.

Reed blew out an exasperated breath. "You're my best friend, Venus," he said more calmly. "And I don't want to see you get hurt."

There it was again. His declaration about them being best friends. He wasn't wrong about it. But lately, every time he brought it up, it seemed like an excuse to drive them apart romantically, and she wanted to stomp her foot in frustration. But she couldn't. She was too dignified and levelheaded and wouldn't get carried away by her emotions like that.

"Thank you for your concern, Reed," she started. "But you have nothing to worry about." Now was her opportunity to tell him she would never care for another man the same way she did him. She had to do it, had to say something before this moment ended and he returned to Lexi.

"But I am worried." He reached for her hands, his expression turning earnest. "I've been thinking about you a lot today…"

Her heart gave an extra thump. Maybe he'd profess his love first after all.

He took a deep breath.

She held herself motionless, eager to hear what he had to say next.

"Venus?"

"Yes?"

"I just want you to find someone who loves you as much as I love Lexi."

She could only stare at him, an ache swelling inside.

"I love her more than anything." His voice dropped a decibel. "She makes me happier than I've been in a long time."

The ache pulsed higher, all the way into Venus's throat. As she studied Reed's face, she could see something that had never been present before. Was it love for Lexi? Was he truly sincere? If he was, how could Venus say anything about her feelings? Doing so would be selfish.

He glanced around, then reached into the inner pocket of his suit coat. "I'm planning to ask her to marry me tonight." He pulled out a black velvet ring box.

Venus knew she needed to act happy and supportive the way a good friend would, but tears pricked the backs of her eyes instead.

"What?" His question was laced with anxiety. "You

don't think I should ask her?"

Here was another chance to tell him no, that she was the one for him instead of Lexi. But how could she say such a thing? Not after all he'd just revealed about being happy.

The bubbling of the fountain filled the silence.

"Say something."

"Sorry. I'm just surprised." She wasn't entirely lying. She *was* surprised by Reed's profession of how happy Lexi made him.

"No, I'm sorry. I should have told you sooner and let you know about my plans." He flipped open the ring box and revealed an emerald-cut diamond ring. It was huge and had to be at least four, if not five, karats.

Seeing the ring made it all so real. Reed had chosen Lexi over her.

"What do you think?" His voice held uncertainty.

"It's stunning."

A smile tugged at the corners of his lips. "She doesn't know anything about it."

Venus doubted that. If the staff of the San Vicente Inn knew, then surely Lexi had some idea of what was happening tonight. But Venus forced herself to nod and smile. "She'll love it."

Reed stared at the ring a moment longer before closing the box and tucking it away in his pocket.

Venus fought against the emotion that was swelling in

her chest. How had this happened? How had she ended up here, with the man she loved excited about marrying another woman?

Reed took a step back. "I'm sorry for getting frustrated about Brock. But I just want what's best for you."

"Of course." If he wanted what was best for her, then why hadn't he chosen her? What was wrong with her that he'd passed her over for someone else? Why didn't he love her the same way she loved him?

"There's one thing I know for certain. Brock McQuaid is *not* right for you. And I don't want you to date him."

Frustration rolled in to mingle with the hurt. Reed didn't want her, so what right did he have to follow her out here and tell her who she could or couldn't date?

"What would you say if I told you not to date Lexi?"

"You wouldn't because there's nothing wrong with Lexi."

Nothing wrong? Venus forced herself not to snort. "I can think of some things that I don't like—"

"You're just saying that because of what I said about Brock."

"She's presumptuous and nosy and overbearing at times."

"What?" Reed's voice rose a notch. "That's not true."

"She posted that picture of me and Brock today even

though Brock told her not to."

"She was just excited."

"She wanted to cause drama."

"Fine." Reed sighed. "She's not perfect. I realize that. But neither am I."

Venus arched her brow, knowing she'd made her point.

"The trouble is," Reed continued in a calmer tone, "you've never been good at picking men to date."

"I can pick guys just fine."

"No, you can't. That's why nothing ever lasts."

Nothing lasted because she'd always compared those guys to him. Had she been wrong to do so and not give them a fair chance?

He studied her face. "You always said you didn't want to be like your mom. But from what I can tell, you're doing the same thing she does."

Her mom had been in and out of relationships as long as Venus could remember and had rejected perfectly great guys because she'd never been able to let go of Marco—Venus's father—in order to love someone else. Reed knew how difficult the subject was for Venus, how much she adored her mom but hated the instability.

"Don't bring up my mom right now, Reed. That's not fair. My dating life is nothing like hers."

"You're afraid of committing—"

"I'm committed to Brock." Even as the words fell out,

she wished she could take them back and tell Reed the truth. But she couldn't. Not now. Not while he was with Lexi. She didn't want to do anything to jeopardize his happiness.

Reed rolled his shoulders and then looked in the direction of the resort. "I've got to get back to the party, to Lexi."

"Don't let me keep you."

He took another step away but hesitated. "I know I can't tell you who you should or shouldn't date. But just be careful, okay?"

"I'll be fine."

He waited another moment before turning and walking away.

He'd made it clear that his choice was Lexi. He'd also made it clear that she, Venus, needed to find someone of her own and that she was pathetic for considering Brock.

Maybe she was pathetic.

Only after he was gone did she sag onto one of the benches and bury her face in her hands and let the tears come.

Had Venus worked up the courage to tell Reed how she really felt?

Brock hovered on the edge of the arboretum near the pathway, waiting for the two to finish their conversation. A part of him was also making sure no one else went out and bothered them, mainly Lexi, who kept glancing toward the path with worried eyes.

At the hard slap of footsteps against the flagstone path, Brock pushed away from the marble statue he'd been leaning against. Reed was coming, and he was alone. That had to mean the conversation hadn't gone well for Venus.

Course, Brock didn't want to jump to any conclusions, but Reed wasn't sporting the happy smile of a man who'd just learned his friend loved him. Instead, he was scowling, and the scowl only got bigger at the sight of Brock.

Brock wasn't sure where all Reed's animosity was coming from. He'd never had any negative interactions with Reed previously. Even if the guy was sometimes uptight and hard-nosed about things, Brock never let that bother him and always did his best to entertain his friends.

As Reed drew up to Brock, he halted and looked like he wanted to take a swing.

Brock guessed the best thing to do in the situation was pretend he didn't notice the strain. "Everything all right with Venus?"

"She's just fine." The words came out in a growl. "And she better stay that way."

Brock forced a grin. "I feel the same way, buddy."

"Good. Because if I ever hear that you've hurt her, you'll wish you'd never looked at her." Reed didn't wait for Brock to respond. Instead, he strode across the span of yard to where Lexi was standing and chatting with several of her cheerleader friends, who had been eyeing Brock since he'd returned from talking with Venus.

They hadn't approached him yet. With the rumors about him and Venus circulating on social media and in the news, maybe fewer women would hit on him tonight, which he wouldn't mind.

Early on in his career, he'd been flattered by all the women who paid him attention, but over the past year, he could admit he'd gotten tired of having to find ways to avoid women without hurting their feelings. He supposed that's why he'd liked being in a relationship with Ainsley Rose. Even if their time together had been mostly superficial, at least he'd gotten a break from the pressure to date.

He watched the path for Venus to make an appearance. He'd wanted to tell her how incredible she looked tonight, but he'd figured so many people flattered her that paying her one more compliment was unoriginal, maybe even as tedious for her as the fan attention was for him.

"You and Venus?" Dallas, one of Reed's bandmates—his lead guitarist—sauntered toward Brock, a bottle of beer in hand. With long brown-gray hair and an equally long beard, the middle-aged man had once played in a heavy-metal band. He was a lady's man—or liked to think he was—and had bonded with Brock over their *lady's man* similarity.

"I'm impressed." Dallas took a swig from his beer.

"Thanks, man." Inwardly Brock sighed. He hadn't known what to tell people about Lexi's post declaring that he and Venus were a *happy couple in love*. Harper had told him to roll with it until they had clear direction on how Venus wanted to handle the situation.

But what exactly did *roll with it* mean? Pretend he was in love with Venus? Acknowledge the congratulations about being a couple?

So far, he'd done both. But he hadn't liked having to lie. It would only make getting out of their fake relationship all the harder.

"Venus Vargas is a goddess." Dallas's eyes were filled with admiration. "You're one lucky dog to finally be the man to win her heart."

"You know me…" Brock forced another grin. "I am a lucky dog."

"Heard she's real picky about who she goes out with. So I reckon she must've lowered her standards if she's willing to be seen with a fellow like you."

Brock laughed, some of the tension easing from his body. He'd always had the philosophy that a person couldn't take himself or life too seriously, that a little laughter and teasing were sometimes the best kind of medicine. He'd even written a song about it early on in his career: "Better Than a Glass of Whiskey."

> Don't pour me another glass of whiskey. Don't hand
>   me another beer.
> Instead, tell me you love me and that you'll always
>   be near.
> It's too easy to get lost in what don't matter, and lose
>   sight of what counts,
> Your smiles and laughter every day and lovin' you
>   all night.

It had been a popular song for a while, earned him some accolades for having depth and heart in his music. If only he could compose his own songs again the way he had at first. Yes, he'd written a song for his brother's engagement recently. He'd thought maybe he'd had a breakthrough in his writer's block, but he hadn't been able to come up with anything meaningful since.

If things didn't change, Steve and BMN had indicated they would hire a songwriter for him.

Having a songwriter was fine for most singers. Reed almost always used songs others wrote for him. But Brock hadn't been able to sing anything that didn't come from himself and his heart. He'd tried, but he just didn't have the same passion or enthusiasm, and it showed.

He had to figure out what was wrong and causing him to be blocked. And he had to do it soon. Because once his world tour ended, he would have a couple of months off the road, and he had to make good use of the time and work on his next album. He'd hoped to have the lyrics written to at least half a dozen songs by now so that he could focus mostly on the music with his band.

But he had nothing…except for Ty's song. After hearing all about Ty and Kinsey's relationship, Brock had been so inspired by their love that he'd written the lyrics and music practically overnight.

Inspired by love. Maybe his critics were right that he didn't know about love. He'd been searching after women to fill him up, but they'd all been wrong and had left him dry, empty, with only dregs at the bottom of his cup.

Those sounded an awful lot like lyrics for a new song.

He straightened and began to fish in his suit pocket for his phone. He had to make a note with his thoughts.

Dallas, in the middle of telling him about one of his latest girlfriends, paused his storytelling and raised a brow.

"Don't mind me." Brock swiped at his phone screen and pulled up his notes app. Quickly he began to type up his thoughts. He might never use the words, but they were the first decent and deep lines he'd come up with in a while. "Just had to get down some sudden inspiration."

"Now that's what I'm talking about!" Dallas's smile widened. "What was the inspiring part? Tanya's pretty smile, or the way she winks at me?"

Brock didn't have the heart to tell Dallas he hadn't heard a single word about Tanya. "Can't say, or it'll ruin the vibes."

"True enough, dog." Dallas slapped him on his arm. "True enough."

At the sight of Venus heading down the path toward him, Brock pocketed his phone. She didn't seem happy. In fact, from the slump of her shoulders and the dip of her chin, she looked miserable. The conversation with Reed must have bombed.

"I'll catch up with you later, Dallas." He turned his back on the guitarist, hoping the guy would get the hint to leave. As he stepped toward Venus, she blotted a finger under first one eye and then the other. Was she wiping away tears?

As she locked in on him, she straightened, picked up her pace, and forced a smile—a practiced smile, one she probably used often in her modeling.

"Hi," she said breezily, as if she didn't have a care in the world.

Maybe that kind of greeting and that kind of smile could fool others, but it wasn't fooling him.

"Wait, Venus." He halted in the middle of the path.

Without faltering in her confident stride, she tried to step around him.

He shifted enough to block her and touched her arm. "Please."

She stopped.

He could feel the tension radiating from her body. Why had he stopped her? What could he possibly say to make her feel better? In a situation like hers, there wasn't anything that could make the heartache go away. Not even the words *I'm sorry* were adequate. They were flimsy, designed to make the person saying them feel better and not the other way around.

He had the sudden urge to write that down on his notes app too. Why was he feeling inspired tonight? He didn't understand it except that there was something about Venus that was making him think more deeply than he had in a while.

She released a long sigh.

Was she exasperated? Did she want to run off and leave him and everyone else behind? If so, he wouldn't blame her.

He had to say something before she did. "Hey," he whispered. "I can't pretend to know what you're going through, but I'm here for you tonight. If you need someone."

She didn't immediately respond. Then she sniffled and nodded. "Thank you, Brock."

"Anytime."

She remained motionless. "Do you mind…would it be okay…could we pretend to be a couple tonight?"

He tried not to startle at her question, but it took him off guard so that he didn't know what to say.

She shook her head and started to move forward. "Never mind. That's selfish of me—"

"No." He tightened his hold on her arm, keeping her in place beside him. "Of course we can stick together."

She stood stiffly for another second, then seemed to relax.

"It would probably be easier," he whispered. "Then we won't have as many questions."

They would still have people asking how they'd gotten together and wondering how serious they were. But it would be simpler to fend off the queries if they were together rather than on opposite ends of the party and hardly speaking to each other.

"I don't think I can handle Reed's pity—or Lexi's," she whispered. "Not tonight."

He offered her his elbow. "I'm all yours tonight, darlin'. You can do anything with me that you want."

For the first time since their unusual encounter earlier, a genuine smile tugged at her lips. "Anything?"

"Promise. Anything."

With a widening smile, she tucked her hand into his elbow and began to stroll forward. "You might come to regret your promise."

He grinned back. "Doubt it. Not with you."

She squeezed his arm. "You are the world's biggest flirt. You do know that, don't you?"

"Course I do."

This time she laughed lightly.

The sky was growing dark with the coming of night, and the decorative lights strung overhead provided a beautiful ambiance to the arboretum. With the open bar and the food tent, everyone seemed happy.

They'd reached the edge of the party again, and the conversations lulled around them at their appearance. Probably because she was so breathtaking that no one could resist staring at her.

Either she pretended not to notice, or she was so used to turning heads that she didn't pay attention to it anymore. She kept her eyes on him, walking with perfected poise. "Thank you for making me laugh."

"Anytime."

She slipped her arms through his more securely and pressed against him, clearly playing up their role as a couple. "Anything? Anytime? You're not only the world's biggest flirt, but you're accommodating enough to be the world's most perfect boyfriend."

"I try."

For a while, they wandered along the edges of the party, managed to eat a little, and thankfully deflected most inquiries about their relationship. He found himself enjoying the time with her like he usually did, and as the party progressed, she seemed to relax.

She'd just finished dipping a strawberry into a chocolate fondue when a camera flashed in their faces. She set aside the chocolate and then peered up at him with wide eyes filled with adoration.

Even though he knew it wasn't real adoration and that she was performing for the photographer Reed had hired, a small part of Brock wished this were real and that she really did adore him. He wasn't sure where that thought came from—maybe from the growing awareness of how empty his relationships had always been and his desire to move beyond that.

Whatever the case, he couldn't read more into her poses—because that's all they were, poses for the camera, something she was an expert at. In fact, it would be better for both of them if he kept things from getting too serious tonight when she was having a hard time over Reed.

As the photographer angled in for another picture, Brock kicked up his crooked grin, the one that earned him the most fan comments. Then before he could stop himself, he bent down and laid a gentle kiss on her forehead. Again, he wasn't sure where that'd come from, but it felt right, like she needed it in the moment.

Her eyes turned glassy, and she looked away, blinking rapidly, all the while maintaining her perfect smile.

"Attention, everybody." Reed's voice suddenly filled the lull. "Could I have your attention, please?"

Immediately, Venus stiffened.

And as the guests all shifted to look at Reed, Reed stuck his hand into his coat pocket and pulled out a small ring box.

So this was it. The big moment.

Reed darted a glance toward Venus, as though making sure she was there and watching. Then he smiled at Lexi and dropped down to one knee in front of her.

She gasped and covered her mouth with her hand, as if she were surprised. Maybe she was.

"Lexi," Reed started. "I've never met another woman like you."

Venus's fingers dug into Brock's arm, and Brock couldn't help but feel irked at Reed's callous statement too.

"You make me the happiest I've ever been," Reed continued as he opened the ring box. "I want to spend the rest of my life with you."

It wasn't a poetic proposal. It wasn't even all that creative. And it was even a little selfish. After all, the relationship wasn't about how happy *she* was making *him*. It ought to be the other way around and about making her the happiest she'd ever been.

Brock's fingers itched again to pull out his phone and jot down the ideas, the lines for a new song.

A thrum of excitement pulsed through him. What was going on? He was starting to find inspiration everywhere. And it was awesome.

"Lexi," Reed continued, "I would be honored if you would agree to marry me."

She waited until the box was open and the ring in sight, then she dropped her hand and gasped again. Her smile was wide and genuine and happy, and her eyes were glassy with tears.

Reed was watching her expectantly.

She nodded and held out her hand. "Yes! Yes! Of course I'll marry you, baby!"

Reed took the ring out and slid it down her finger. All the while, the photographer was capturing every moment of the proposal.

Brock felt Venus tremble against him, and he brought up his other hand and laid it over hers on his arm.

She glanced at him, giving him a glimpse of the despair in her eyes.

He squeezed her hand, hoping to reassure her that he was there for her.

Reed and Lexi embraced, then kissed. As they did so, the rest of the guests clapped and cheered, all except for him and Venus. Instead, she held herself stiffly, her smile gone.

When the kissing was done and everyone had toasted the happy couple, Venus began to tug free. She'd done her duty and stayed for the proposal. Now that it was over, was she running off?

He wouldn't blame her if she wanted to leave. Maybe he'd go too.

"Ready?" he whispered as he took a step backward.

She hesitated. "Ready for what?"

"I'm getting out of here. How about you?"

She nodded. "Yes."

Keeping her securely by his side, he turned to go.

"Hold on, Venus!" Reed's voice carried above the crowd. "Don't leave yet."

Under the glow of the little lights above them, her face looked especially pale, and her eyes held a panic that told him she didn't want to stay.

Brock tossed a grin over his shoulder. "Hey now. It's our last night together. We deserve a little time alone, don't we?"

His comment was met with laughter from everyone except Reed. The guy forced a smile, but Brock was beginning to think Reed was jealous.

Reed's eyes said it all. He was marrying Lexi, but Venus was his too, and he was making sure no one else could claim her.

Brock's gut tightened. The guy was a selfish son of a gun. As far as Brock was concerned, Venus was better off without him.

"Venus," Reed called again. "My best friend in the whole world."

Curving her lips up into a bright smile, one that didn't reach her eyes, she spun to face Reed.

Reed held out a hand as though he expected Venus to trot over to him like a hound dog begging for attention. "I would love it if you would agree to stand up with me at my wedding as my best woman."

With all eyes turning upon her, Venus didn't waver. She kept her perfect smile, her perfect pose, her perfect composure. "Of course, Reed. I would be honored."

Reed smiled back. "I couldn't do it without you."

She didn't respond except to nod at him graciously.

Lexi latched on to Reed's arm as though to draw his attention back to her. "Everyone here is invited to the wedding. We're having it in two months at Reed's family's home." Which was an oceanfront mansion that had a private beach.

"Two months?" Venus's whisper sounded strangled.

Obviously the engagement wasn't a surprise for Lexi if she'd already been planning the wedding. So why bother to have a party? What was the point?

"Let's go." Venus tugged Brock back around. She couldn't seem to leave the party fast enough. When they were inside the inn and well away from the party goers, she halted, released him, and bent over.

He wanted to ask her if she was okay, but he knew that was a stupid question. She was upset about not only the engagement but Reed involving her in the wedding party and the ceremony happening so soon.

Was there anything—anything at all—he could do for her?

As if hearing his unspoken question, she straightened and looked directly at him. "Let's do this."

He quirked a brow. "Do what?"

"Have your people talk to my people, and let's work out an arrangement to have a relationship." The hurt in her eyes said it all, that Reed had injured her not only as a woman but also as a friend.

"I know what's in this for me," he said slowly. "I'll get to maybe repair my reputation. But what's in it for you?"

"If I don't do this, Reed will assume I'm breaking up with you because he told me to. And I don't want to give him that satisfaction."

"He told you to break up with me?" This

conversation was the strangest and most confusing he'd ever had.

"He said you're a player and can't make a commitment."

"Ouch." Even if Reed's description was slightly true, the comment still stung. Probably because it echoed what his family thought of him—that he was the wild child of the family. "Maybe I just haven't met the right woman."

"Well, how about if I'm that right woman?"

A fake right woman. But what did it matter? "So you want to do this to prove something to Reed?"

"I don't want his pity. Just because he found someone doesn't mean I can't."

Brock scratched the back of his head. The conversation was only getting more confusing by the second. "So you want to be in a fake relationship with me to prove to Reed that you can find someone?"

"Yes, exactly." She held his gaze, her eyes bright. "If he can find happiness with someone else, so can I."

"Except you won't really be happy with me because it will all be pretend."

"He won't know that."

Brock dropped his hand and stuffed both into his pockets. He didn't like the idea of having a bogus relationship with Venus for any reason at all, not for her sake or his. But if she wanted it, he'd do it.

She was watching him expectantly.

He offered her a grin. "How long will we be in this fake relationship?"

She expelled a breath. "Our people can connect, and they can work out all the details." Then she started down the hallway, away from him toward the elevators.

He was tempted to follow after her and ask her if he could take her out tonight. Instead, he just stood unmoving and watched her beautiful sway.

When she reached the elevator, she glanced back at him. "Thank you, Brock. I wish you all the best."

The elevator opened, and she disappeared inside.

Her words lingered in the air, sounding a lot like goodbye. Strangely, he found that he didn't want to say goodbye yet to Venus Vargas.

6

"I like Brock McQuaid," Mom called from her spot on the paddock fence.

Venus slid her hand over the mane of her quarter horse, a stunning gold-champagne color and aptly named Goldie. The afternoon light not only made the mare shine but glistened off the lush greenery of the manicured shrubs and gardens all around the paddock and barn.

Nestled against the Santa Monica range, the sprawling ranch was known for its winery and also had a wedding venue on part of the property. Mom paid people to take care of everything for her, including the horses, the barns, and the house a short distance from the barns, which was constructed of smooth stucco with a red terra-cotta roof and arched doorways and windows.

What kind of answer could she give to Mom when everything with Brock McQuaid was entirely fabricated? She didn't want to lie, but Mom still had too many friends in important places and had never been good about keeping secrets.

"I always thought you'd end up with Reed." Mom swung her workworn cowboy boots, her tight jeans outlining her nearly perfect body. With a cute baseball cap and long blond braids, Mom looked like she could be Venus's sister, even though she was double Venus's twenty-four years.

Mom was still as beautiful today as she'd been as a model. She'd never risen to the stardom and popularity that Venus had, but she'd always been a knockout and still was—of course with a little help from Botox.

"Reed really does love Lexi." Venus had been thinking about the engagement party since sneaking away last night, and she'd come to the same conclusion that she had at the party. Reed cared about Lexi, and Lexi loved him in return.

Mom gave a whistle as she looked at her phone screen—probably still scrolling through pictures of Venus and Brock at the engagement party, more pictures that Lexi had posted to her social media. "Well, I'd take Brock McQuaid as a replacement, that's for sure."

Last night, after she'd walked away from Brock, Venus had gone directly to her room, packed her bags, and driven the couple of hours to her mom's ranch near Malibu. She'd needed the time with her mom and her horses and had decided to spend the extra days off at the ranch before flying back to Europe.

Thankfully, Mom was between boyfriends and had been home when Venus had arrived after midnight. They'd stayed up late talking mostly about Reed, had slept in, and now Venus was enjoying some time with her horses—or trying to.

She was still irritated at Reed for the way he'd sprung the engagement on her and how he'd also put her on the spot to be his best woman. She was also irritated that he'd compared her love life to her mom's. It had been callous and inconsiderate, especially because he knew how different she wanted to be.

Just because she'd gone out with lots of men and hadn't had a steady boyfriend or dated anyone seriously didn't mean she was turning into her mom. She'd just been waiting for Reed, and now that he'd obviously rejected her, she would show him that she could be in a relationship. Even more than that, she'd show him that he was wrong about her being afraid of commitment. She would stay committed to her fake relationship for as long as it took to prove to Reed she wasn't pathetic. Except the whole plan to fake date Brock was the epitome of pathetic, wasn't it?

She released a tight breath. "It's not serious with Brock."

"It doesn't have to be, honey." Mom finally tucked her phone into her pocket. "Sometimes I think you need to lighten up a little."

Like you? The words pressed for release, but Venus bit them back. She hadn't come to the ranch to argue with her mom. She'd come to get away from Reed, and yes, maybe nurse her broken heart a little.

"I can't see Brock getting too serious either," Mom offered. "Not after his track record of moving on from one woman to the next."

Kind of like Mom's record of moving on from one boyfriend to the next. But again, Venus forced herself to stay silent. It had never done any good to point out her mom's failures with men. It never changed anything because her mom always found someone new, always went all in with the guy to the point of being obsessed. But those relationships never lasted more than a year, most a lot less.

Venus had her theories about why, mainly that Mom was still in love with Marco, her first love and Venus's father. Mom had met him when she'd been in Italy on a photo shoot. Marco was from a wealthy family who had a fortune in banking and jewelry. To Marco, Mom had been just a fling, a beautiful American model he could see whenever she was in the country. But Mom had made him her whole world.

Although Mom had never said so, she'd hoped Marco would come live in America with her on her family's ranch, especially since her parents were deceased and she was alone. She'd even been willing to sell the ranch and move to Rome to marry Marco.

It had taken a couple of years and the pregnancy with Venus for Mom to realize Marco wasn't willing to rearrange his life for her. He'd blamed his family, claiming they wanted him to marry a good Italian from among their social circles.

In the end, he'd married someone else, and Mom had been left to raise a baby by herself. Even though Mom didn't need Marco's financial support because she had her family's money, Marco had been decent enough to provide for Venus over the years.

Venus had met him twice in her life, and that was enough for her. Once had been as a young girl when he was visiting Los Angeles. All she remembered from that time was that he was tall and handsome and Mom had been giddy around him.

The other time had been on a photo shoot in Rome, and she'd asked him if he wanted to have dinner. He'd been busy, but he'd made time for drinks. The meeting had been awkward, and Venus had walked away from it satisfied that she hadn't missed anything by not having her father in her life.

Regardless of the loser that she thought Marco was, her mom had never stopped loving him. He'd been her first love and obviously her last.

"I say just enjoy having a fling with Brock McQuaid,"

Mom said with a flash of a smile. "Take all you can of that hotty while he's around."

"Sure, Mom." Venus had long ago learned not to take dating advice from her mom. In fact, Venus had half a mind to call her agent and let Kristin know she'd changed her mind about being in a relationship with Brock. It wasn't too late. His assistant had only just contacted Kristin this morning about coming up with a plan for the fake dating.

Venus had read through Ainsley Rose's accusations again—her claims that Brock didn't want to get serious, that he didn't know how to love, and that he wasn't ready for a committed relationship. Venus didn't know whether to believe her. But whether the pop star's accusations were true or not, a part of Venus wanted to help Brock out of his tight spot, especially after how nice he'd been to her last night.

Venus sighed, then urged Goldie into a canter and let the warm Malibu sunshine bathe her face.

Mom hopped from her perch. "On the other hand, it's important to give each new man a chance to find out where things could lead. You never know if you don't explore the possibilities."

Give men a chance? Venus almost scoffed. Her mom gave too many men a chance, and Venus meant what she'd told Reed, that she wanted to be different from her mom.

"It's not serious, Mom. Brock's a nice guy, and we like each other's company. That's about it."

A text pinged. One with the special chime she used for Reed's texts.

Venus didn't want to feel the tug to see what he had to say, but the need to hear from him had been nagging at her. She'd left without a word, and he'd been silent ever since. Was he angry with her? She didn't want to cause a rift, but she didn't know how to smooth things over.

She reined in Goldie and at the same time tugged her phone from her back pocket.

As she touched her screen, Reed's text came to life:

Reed: *I'm sorry for the things I said last night and not trusting you.*

She could feel the tension ease from her shoulders. They'd had very few arguments over the years, and she was glad that Reed was always quick to patch things up.

Venus: *I'm sorry too.*

Reed: *You know I just care about you.*

Venus: *I know.*

Reed: *I'll do better to support you in your relationship with Brock.*

Venus paused her fingers above the keyboard. Did she want Reed to support her relationship with Brock? Not really. But what could she say now?

She scrambled for a response but couldn't think of anything coherent. Finally, she typed a lame text:

Venus: *Thanks. That means a lot.*

Reed: *Still friends?*

Venus: *Of course.*

Reed: *I'll always need you.*

Always need her? What did that really mean to him?

That wasn't the first time he'd said something like that. Once upon a time she would have interpreted those words to mean that he wanted to be with her long term, that they had a future together.

But now? His engagement had changed everything.

She blew out an exasperated breath. He didn't really need her. At least, not the way she'd hoped and believed he would.

Reed: *I hope you'll always need me too.*

Venus: *I will.*

Things would have to change between them. But she was relieved that Reed wanted some things to be the same. She didn't like that he'd gotten engaged to someone else. But at least she could cling to the hope that he still cared about her too.

Venus hadn't been feeling the energy for the photo shoot since it'd started, and she wasn't sure why.

"Relax, Venus." The photographer was sprawled out on the ground now, his lens pointed up.

Venus tried to soften her expression. She didn't want wrinkle lines, especially not while modeling a new makeup line for Fitzsimmons SYA Beauty, one of the most expensive brands in the world, at the Fitzsimmons headquarters on the Champs-Élysées in Paris.

But she had been feeling the tension ever since Kristin had stepped into the photo shoot a short while ago and informed her that she had a date with Brock when she finished.

"More." The photographer kept the lens pointed at her face. "S'il vous plaît, ma chérie."

Again, Venus attempted to let the tension ease from her body. She shifted into a new pose under the studio light and against the cityscape backdrop, one of Paris along the Seine River. The room was full of the usual people on the fringes of the set—assistants, set designers, makeup artists, hair stylists, wardrobe stylists, and more. Most of them were quietly watching her.

She was used to being scrutinized, and today was no different...except that she'd been tired all week since Reed's engagement last weekend. And she hadn't been expecting to meet with Brock tonight. That had come from out of nowhere.

The photographer lowered his camera and pushed himself up to a sitting position. "I think we should call it a day, no?"

"Yes, I agree." Venus hated to end a photo shoot on a negative note, but it was getting late, and she was already running behind for the dinner with Brock. She took a step away from the backdrop and out from underneath the lights.

She could see the Fitzsimmons representative scowling and starting toward her. Venus ducked her head and lengthened her stride toward the dressing room. "That's all for tonight. Thank you, everyone. I'll see you tomorrow." She spoke the words over her shoulder without hesitating in her stride.

As she stepped into her dressing room, she closed the door behind her on anyone who might try to follow her. She leaned back against it, dragging in a breath through the tight confines of the formfitting gown. It was a stunning dress that Fitzsimmons had given her as part of the photo shoot, a sleek floor-length creation that was made up of gold beaded fringes throughout. Its square neckline and slim bodice fit her to perfection.

With her golden hair curled and falling over her shoulders, the new warm tones of the eyeshadow made her blue eyes even bluer, so that the photos had been some of her best to date—or at least, the photos from earlier.

"There's no time to change, Venus," came Kristin's voice from outside. "Besides, what you have on will work."

She didn't want Brock to think she was trying to impress him. That was actually the last thing she wanted to do. Even so, she added a spritz of perfume, reapplied her lip gloss, then found the clutch that matched the gown and filled it with a few personal items.

When she opened the dressing-room door, the studio had emptied, thankfully.

"Once-a-week dates with Brock are too much." Venus crossed toward the hallway that would lead to the rear exit of the stately building.

Kristin followed behind. "Brock's manager insisted that you make appearances together once a week. You know that."

Venus's heels clicked on the tile floor. Once she was

finished with the shoot in the studio tomorrow, she was flying to Cannes in the French Riviera for another shoot on the beaches to get a more natural setting.

She'd planned on relaxing in her hotel room tonight after the long day of being on her feet. But somehow she'd been scheduled to have dinner with Brock in order to prove to the whole world that they were still dating…because clearly, a week without seeing each other was cause for concern.

She sighed with exasperation. "Why the worry? Everyone knows we're both busy with our separate lives."

The tap of Kristin's heels echoed behind Venus. Her agent, in a stylish suit, was tall too, and thankfully always able to keep up. "Since we leaked the news about your dating Brock to the press, neither of you have said a word. That's not exactly proving you're in a happy and loving relationship."

"Well, that's because we're not." Venus hadn't spoken with Brock since she'd walked away from him after the engagement party.

"You have to act like it."

She halted abruptly and faced Kristin. "Should I just put an end to the charade?"

As a former model, Kristin was still graceful and lovely even though, at thirty-five, her features and body were no longer considered young enough. Instead, she'd turned her experience into being an agent, one of the best employed with IMG, New York's top modeling agency.

"The wheels are already set in motion," Kristin said carefully, used to dealing with emotional young women. "If you put a halt to things now, it won't look good for either you or Brock."

Not to mention she'd make a fool of herself with Reed after telling him that she was committed to Brock. After Reed had texted and let her know that he would do better to support her relationship with Brock, how could she break things off now?

"You're right. I have to drag this out for a little longer."

"At least three months."

"Right." Three months was the timeline Brock's people and her people had come up with. Along with the once-a-week dates, a weeklong vacation was thrown in there somewhere during the three months. Also, she and Brock were to be each other's plus-one to all events, with the exclusion of family gatherings so that they didn't put their families in the middle of the charade.

"We all agreed that you would both need to do enough to make the relationship seem believable."

"And so you're saying I'm not doing enough?"

Kristin didn't blink at the direct question. Instead, she met Venus's gaze with a directness of her own, which was a quality Venus appreciated about her agent. "Already, people here in Paris are saying they haven't seen any evidence you're in love."

Venus scoffed. "How exactly do they know that? Is there a certain way a person in love acts? Especially when they're not with their significant person?"

"I suppose so."

"How?"

"They call or text that person whenever they can."

She had noticed Brock hadn't been calling or texting or pretending to have a real relationship. She hadn't wanted him to make more of their agreement. On the other hand, she had expected him to show a little more interest, even if just a tiny bit. Any other man would have. So why not him?

A part of her already knew the answer. Brock McQuaid wasn't like other men.

"Anything else I should be doing?"

"You can act a little excited when someone mentions Brock's name."

"What? No. That's silly."

"Then you can talk about him some, bring up his name, act like you can't wait until you see him."

"That's all ridiculous. I wouldn't do that in a real relationship, and I certainly don't want to do it in a fake one."

"Then at least when you're out to dinner tonight, act as though you're happy to be with him."

Venus released a tight breath. She wasn't happy about

it, but she could see the point in at least projecting an image that she was. If there was one thing she was good at, it was projecting an image she wanted people to see.

"Fine. I'll do my best." She turned a corner and made her way down a flight of steps. As she exited through Fitzsimmons's back door onto the side street, she stopped short at the sight of a limousine waiting in the shadows instead of her usual chauffeur.

She lifted a brow at Kristin, who stood in the open door.

"It was Brock's idea."

"You mean his assistant's idea."

"No, I talked to him, and he's the one who arranged it."

"Oh." Venus had ridden in limos before to awards ceremonies, red carpet galas, and opening events, but never to dinner.

She studied the long, sleek vehicle for a sign of Brock.

"He's meeting you at Maxim's," Kristin said, as if seeing inside her mind.

A part of Venus wished he were waiting for her in the car and that they could have a private moment before being subjected to the scrutiny of every other guest and waitstaff at Maxim's. But what would she say to him? It wasn't like they were really dating.

"After you're seated"—Kristin's voice dropped low—"I'll leak word to the paparazzi that the two of you are having dinner together at Maxim's."

Venus didn't like that idea, but it was a necessary evil. They had to be spotted together, a couple in love. Otherwise, what was the point of going out?

"You'll get a few pictures together leaving the restaurant, then ride back to the hotel. He's staying at Plaza Athénée too."

She hadn't taken Brock for the sort of man who would not only go to Maxim's but also stay at the Hôtel Plaza Athénée. Only a short distance from Champs-Élysées, it was convenient to Fitzsimmons, Dior, Cartier, Louis Vuitton, Gucci, Chanel, Tiffany & Co., and other stores that she'd modeled for over recent years. Not only that, but every time she stepped into Plaza Athénée, she felt like she was royalty and visiting one of her palaces. The antiques and the decor and furnishings were beautiful but in a decidedly nineteenth-century way.

"Tell Brock's people he can stay where he usually does."

Kristin just shook her head. "We already decided it would be best for the two of you to be at the same hotel since that's what normal dating couples would do."

Normal dating couples would probably even share the same room. But after watching her mom casually sleep with so many men in an attempt to help her forget about her one true love, Venus had vowed she would never sleep with anyone except the man she married. She'd been clear about that to all the men she'd dated. She supposed that had something to do with why she limited the number of dates she went on, because most men pressured her for more than she was willing to give.

Whatever the case, it wouldn't bother her if Brock stayed at the Plaza Athénée. They would return and go their separate ways, and that's all there was to it.

She crossed to the limo and paused to study her reflection in the mirrorlike tinted window. A strange twinge of unease breezed over her. She fingered the low neckline of her gown and then one of her long waves.

How was it that a woman like her, who had nearly everything, couldn't manage to earn the love of the man she wanted? What was wrong with her?

"Brock's a terrific guy and a good sport," Kristin said from the doorway. "Don't take this too seriously, and just go and let yourself have a little fun."

Venus nodded. Yes, that's what she'd do. She'd enjoy a dinner out, try to have fun, and then she could forget all about Brock until next week.

During the short ride to Maxim's, she could feel herself relaxing. Kristin had been right about Brock being a terrific guy and a good sport. No other man had ever sent a limo to pick her up for dinner, not even Reed. And Reed could definitely afford it. Not only did he have his own money from his country music career, but his family was almost as wealthy as hers.

Not that Reed should have sent a limo for her. Why would he make such a grand gesture for a friend? Brock was only doing it to pretend to be in love with her so that he could repair his image, which hadn't improved over the past week. From what she could tell from the little she'd read on social media, everyone was still saying the same things, questioning why he was singing about love when he didn't really know what it was.

He needed tonight to look authentic, and he needed their relationship to be more visible. She could do that for him, couldn't she?

The limo pulled up in front of Maxim's, and she was ushered out under the red awning. She half expected Brock to be waiting for her so that he could draw the attention of fans and get more exposure for the "happy couple in love." But he wasn't anywhere visible as the maître d' led her through the exquisitely decorated restaurant.

The elegant restaurant on Rue Royale didn't seem to be Brock's style, but it was hers—and Reed's. They'd gone on occasion and had enjoyed the iconic restaurant that had catered to celebrities, politicians, and other elite since 1893.

Filled with artwork on every wall and in every corner, the restaurant was a masterpiece unto itself. The furniture was all dark mahogany with red velvet surrounded by beveled mirrors, bronze foliage, stained glass, wall frescoes, and more.

The low lighting created a romantic ambiance, as did the live music coming from the bar. The tables were all full, as usual, the crystal and silver gleaming, the waft of lobster and roasted chicken in the air.

As she wound through the restaurant, most of the other guests refrained from staring at her. Since so many celebrities dined there, perhaps they were used to seeing popular faces. It was also possible that people might not know exactly who she was, even if they did recognize her face.

In a far corner, slightly more secluded than the others, Brock was already seated. He was most definitely noticeable in his three-piece suit, this one a medium blue. With his hair styled back and a slight layer of dark scruff on his face, he still looked rugged, like the cowboy at heart he claimed to be and was quite possibly the best-looking man in the entire restaurant.

As if sensing her presence, or perhaps simply checking for her to arrive, he glanced up from his phone. At the sight of her, he pushed back from the table and stood, slipping his phone away. He offered her his disarming, crooked grin at the same time that his dark eyes swept over her.

Oh, those eyes. Oh, oh, oh. Every time she saw Brock, the thick, warm brown won her over. They were slay-me-now eyes that had the power to make a woman forget her own name. Not her. They didn't have that power over her. But there was a reason he'd made *People* magazine's "Sexiest Man Alive" issue last year.

He stepped toward her as though he meant to embrace her. Like a real dating couple would do after a week apart. But then he hesitated.

They absolutely had to hug. There couldn't be a moment of hesitation, not even in Maxim's, where most people were trying to ignore them and their reunion.

Instead of waiting for him to initiate, she closed the distance between them, wrapped her arms around him, and embraced him the way any girlfriend would.

8

Venus was as stunning as the last time he'd seen her. If it were possible, she was even more striking with her hair flowing in long waves, her eyes wider and bluer than he'd ever seen them before, and her gown shimmering.

And she was hugging him.

He'd told himself that he needed to do as Harper had coached him before coming into the restaurant. He had to treat Venus better than any woman he'd ever gone out with, had to display the right amount of physical affection, and needed to look at her as if his whole world revolved around her. If he could do those things, Harper claimed, he might be able to convince the skeptical press that he really was in love.

Otherwise, he was in a losing battle, because currently, everyone was saying his relationship with Venus was superficial, just like with all his past women.

He hated the prospect of having to lie through the

whole evening, but he'd gotten himself into this mess with Venus and now had to bide his time until the three months of their fake relationship expired.

He wrapped his arms around her in return, pulling her close. "Hey there, darlin'. It's good to see you." He was relieved that much was honest. He *was* glad to see her. She'd filled a pretty big portion of his thoughts throughout the week, and he hadn't exactly been sure why. Maybe because she'd been devastated the previous weekend but had tried to be brave about it. Maybe because Reed had been callous to her about the whole engagement. And maybe because he'd witnessed a softer side to her than he'd seen before, and, well, he'd liked that side.

He guessed a real dating couple would probably kiss when they pulled apart, and he'd been telling himself that he'd dip in and press a brief kiss on her lips and that it wouldn't mean anything other than doing what Harper had instructed him to do.

But as she began to pull back, he released her all the way and couldn't make himself steal a kiss. If and when he kissed her, he wanted her consent first.

For now, no matter the rumors or the gossip, he wanted to treat her the way she deserved—with respect and consideration—which obviously had been lacking to some degree in her *friendship* with Reed. Was it because Reed took her for granted? Brock hadn't been able to figure out the dynamics even though he'd tried.

For tonight, none of that was important. Nothing else mattered but being fully present with Venus.

He stood back and held her at arm's length. He swept his gaze over her, noting the way the elegant dress fit every curve of her body. But he didn't linger on her appearance and instead focused on her smile. "I just love your smile, darlin'. And I'm glad I get to see it again."

Her lips shifted slightly, curling up higher and losing some of the stiffness. At the same time, her eyes seemed to shine a little brighter.

Had he made her happy? Was her smile genuine now? He hoped so.

She dropped her gaze to his mouth. "I'm glad to see your smile again too."

"What? This old thing?" He cocked up one side the way women liked.

She laughed lightly, and he liked that he'd been the cause of it.

She allowed him to help her into her chair, and then he took his place across from her.

He could admit that the few times he'd been in Paris, he'd never dined at Maxim's. While it wasn't his usual style, an elegant, upscale place like this didn't intimidate him since he'd grown up going to fancy dinners at the Cliffside Dining Room at his family's ranch. Of course, the Cliffside was no Maxim's, but his mom had made sure he'd learned proper manners for a formal dinner.

Their server brought them a plate of gougères, poured them a signature cocktail, took their meal selections, and then left them alone. Even with the low hum of conversations around them as well as the live music spilling into the room, their table still felt private.

"How was your week?" Venus asked politely after she took a sip of her drink.

"Busy with two concerts—one in Oslo and the other in Stockholm."

She placed her glass down and turned her attention on him. With all that beauty directed his way, he felt like he was looking directly at the sun and needed sunglasses to keep from being dazzled.

"I'd love to hear about your concerts," she said. "What were they like?"

For a few minutes, he told her about the venues, the sold-out shows, the bands doing his opening acts, and the problem he'd had when one of his backup singers had shown up for the performance drunk.

As he finished, she was sitting forward, leaning closer to him across the table, her eyes wide with interest, her face so beautiful he half couldn't believe he was sitting with her having dinner.

"So what did you do? Fire him?"

"Her. And yep. Unfortunately it wasn't the first time she's shown up at a sound check that way."

"Then this was her second chance?"

He ducked his head. "More like her fourth or fifth."

Venus didn't respond.

He glanced up to see her smiling another smile that reached her eyes. "Brock McQuaid, you're a big softy."

For some reason her words settled inside him like warm honey butter on a fresh-baked corn muffin. "Figure since God's given me as much as He has, I've got more responsibilities, and that means taking good care of all the people who work for me."

"That's very noble of you."

"It's the right thing. Which is why I sent her back to the States and offered to pay for her rehab, if she's willing to go."

Venus reached out a hand and captured his where he was twisting the stem of his wine glass. "Every time I see you, you surprise me more." Her fingers were slender and cool…and they were elegant, just like everything about her. She squeezed his hand and started to lift hers away.

Before she could do so, he captured her fingers, not letting her get away. "Suppose I don't have the best reputation."

"The only thing the media cares to report on is how many women you've been with, not the stories that really matter like this one with your backup singer."

Brock shrugged. "That's partly because I like to keep those kinds of things private. Figured it's nobody's business what my backup singer's doing and how I'm involved in helping her."

"True."

He met her gaze again, and he liked the admiration that was directed at him. "Hey, I'm no saint, that's for sure. Just ask my band. They'll tell you about all my flaws."

"Maybe I will ask them." Her voice held a teasing note.

"Maybe you should." The moment he spoke the words, he had the sudden need to have Venus come to one of his concerts. She'd occasionally gone to Reed's. Brock knew that because Reed always posted a selfie with her whenever she was there.

Before she could pull her hand free, he clasped hers more eagerly. "Come this week."

"Oh, I couldn't—"

"I have a concert in Reykjavík and one in Berlin. If you're anywhere in the neighborhood, I'd love for you to be there."

"I'll be down in Cannes for four or five days before heading back to New York."

"Stop over in Berlin on your way home."

"I have several shoots waiting for me."

"Let them wait an extra day."

This time she didn't immediately say no, which filled him with a ridiculous amount of hope. She was watching his face. Was she trying to gauge his sincerity? Whether he was doing this to play up their relationship or because he really wanted her to come?

"This has nothing to do with the—" He wasn't exactly sure how to refer to their dating agreement. He didn't want to say anything about it in such a public place because there was no telling who was listening. On the other hand, he wanted her to know he was sincere about asking her to come. "Let's put it this way. I'd invite you even if you weren't my girlfriend."

She tilted her head, the candlelight on the table highlighting her cheekbones and the sleek lines of her jaw and chin.

"I promise it'll be an experience you won't forget."

"How so?"

"Because my concerts are always unforgettable."

"A tad arrogant, are we?"

"Just honest." And yes, arrogant. But if arrogance got her to come, then he didn't care.

"That will be two dates in one week."

"I don't mind if you don't." When his agent had laid out the plans for his fake relationship with Venus, he could admit he'd been a little disappointed they weren't seeing each other more often. Once a week wasn't much. And neither was a weeklong vacation.

Then again, he didn't want to facilitate too much closeness and, in doing so, lead her on.

She hesitated.

He offered her another one of his killer smiles. "Pretty please with sugar on top."

Her eyes filled with humor. "You're difficult to resist."

"Are you saying I'm irresistible?"

"Not at all. I certainly wouldn't want to puff you up even more."

He chuckled. "Don't worry. That's not possible."

She laughed lightly too. "Fine. I'll come."

"Good." Satisfaction wafted through him. "You won't regret it."

As their server brought them a cheese soufflé appetizer, they talked more about his concerts and his tour. After being involved in Reed's career, she was much more knowledgeable than most people about the life of a country music singer.

With each new course, they continued to talk easily about all that they had going on in their lives. She shared about her few days so far in Paris modeling for Fitzsimmons's new makeup line. He didn't know as much about all that she did and found himself eager to learn more about her modeling.

Of course, because her mother had been a model, Venus had grown up hearing all about it and had started off doing child modeling for GUESS and other smaller brands. She said she hadn't planned on making a career out of modeling, had intended to pursue a business degree so that she could eventually have her own fashion business. But her freshman year of college, she'd been approached by IMG with an offer that was too difficult to turn down. So she'd dropped out of school six years ago and had been modeling ever since. She still eventually wanted to have her own clothing and makeup line, but she'd been too busy to make it happen.

In turn, she asked him how he'd become interested in country music. Although he'd finished college with a degree in communications, he'd been singing and playing guitar for most of his life. It had been during his junior year of college, while performing at one of the country fairs in Colorado, that a video of one of his performances had gone viral. After that, he'd been approached by several Nashville labels.

The dinner and the time together passed too quickly—at least from Brock's perspective. When they finished their desert of tarte Tatin, with a generous layer of apples and caramel sauce, she only yawned once, but it was enough to know she was tired from her long day.

When he suggested they call an end to their night, she didn't protest, and for some reason, he wished she would suggest getting coffee or taking a walk along the Seine or visiting the Eiffel Tower lit up at night.

But she was quiet as they made their way through the restaurant. As the front doors of Maxim's opened, a barrage of camera lights flashed in their faces.

He should have guessed Harper would tip off the paparazzi that they were dining together at Maxim's. After all, it was important that Brock be seen with Venus.

"It's showtime," he whispered as he leaned against her. "Are you okay if I give you a side hug?"

In response, she slipped her arm around him and laid her head against his shoulder. She peered up at him with half-lidded eyes and a seductive smile.

His heart flipped with unexpected desire. Their relationship was supposed to be pretend, their interactions staged. But as he gazed back down at her, he found that he didn't have to work hard at pretending to adore her. From her willingness to go along with the charade to her enjoyable company, she'd been the perfect date in every way.

The paparazzi had been roped off on either side of the restaurant walkway, and as he slipped his arm around her back in return and they made their way past the dozens of cameras and people shouting out questions, he held her gaze, unable to let her go.

When they reached the limo, the chauffeur was waiting for them with an open door. Instead of releasing him and ducking inside, Venus paused and lifted up to whisper in his ear. "Kiss me." Her whisper was demanding and sent a shot of heat through him—a heat he knew he shouldn't feel but that sizzled along his nerves anyway.

"It's what they want to see." She nuzzled his ear, then angled in so that he would have easy access to her mouth.

Holy smokes. He was in trouble. He started to shake his head, still unwilling to go that far and be that intimate in a pretend relationship. But before he could back away, she reached up and touched her mouth to his.

In that moment, it was like sparks fanning onto dry windfall. Her lips against his, even though light, were scorching hot, setting his world on fire.

Standing in flames, he was helpless but to kiss her back. He shifted so he could fit his mouth to hers, and in the next instant they were mingling and meshing in graceful and yet intense rhythm.

She was incredible and tasted of apples and champagne. And he couldn't get enough. He wanted to wrap both arms around her and never let her go. The urge was so unexpected and unusual that he broke the kiss as suddenly as it had started.

For a fraction of a moment, a measure of panic sliced through him. Never let go? He couldn't feel that way about Venus, not so quickly and strongly.

She pulled back from him, her lashes still low, hiding whatever she might be feeling in response to the kiss. Which was probably nothing because it was pretend.

As she pivoted away from him and ducked into the

limo, he sucked in a sharp breath and tried to mentally stamp out all the flames that were burning in his body. He had to put out the fire, couldn't let the heat spread, couldn't make more of the kiss than it was—a show for the paparazzi and ultimately for his fans so he could prove to them and everyone that he had more substance than they realized.

Other than that, he wasn't planning to get carried away with Venus, just like he hadn't gotten carried away with any other woman. He was waiting for that one special woman to come along with a strong and passionate love that would last forever, just like it had for his dad and Ty and other McQuaid men. And Venus wasn't that woman. How could she be when she was only a shooting star in his life, burning brightly for a short while but eventually soaring on to a different universe?

He watched her disappear into the limo before he flashed a grin at the paparazzi, one he hoped communicated that he'd thoroughly enjoyed kissing Venus—which was no lie.

The camera flashes nearly blinded him, and the shouts only grew louder. "Is it true you purchased an engagement ring?" "When are you popping the big question?" "Isn't this rather soon?"

Brock didn't bother answering the slew of questions and instead slid inside the limo onto the seat beside Venus. A second later, the door closed, shutting out the crowd and casting them into shadows and silence.

Venus didn't move.

He sat motionless too, not sure what to say or do after a kiss like that. Even after he'd tried to put out the flames, his body still felt scorched.

As the chauffeur took his place and then began to drive away, Venus sat stiffly, the dim light outlining her face. She was staring out the opposite window and didn't look too happy.

He wanted to reach for her hand and make some sort of connection with her, but he crossed his arms instead. "I'm sorry about the onslaught from the paparazzi. I thought you knew—"

"Yes, I knew." Her voice was tinged with irritation. "But what I didn't know was that they would assume we're getting engaged."

"To be honest, I didn't know that was part of the plan either."

"There must be a reason they think that."

"I did go to a jewelry store this afternoon," he continued. "But only to buy a birthday present for my mom."

"Now the whole world believes you went ring shopping for me."

His mind began to whirl. Ella Mae had reminded him of his mom's birthday in a few weeks and had suggested he stop at a couple of places, including a jewelry shop.

What if Harper had started the rumor about him buying an engagement ring? Brock wouldn't put it past his savvy manager.

With his elbows propped on his knees, he groaned and buried his face in his hands. "This has to be my people's fault. Probably attempting to move things along between us more quickly."

She didn't respond.

A heaviness settled over his heart. He should have known something like this might happen. Maybe he never should have agreed to the whole plan to fake date Venus. He didn't like all the lying and deceiving and pretending. Would it have been better for him to simply admit to Ainsley Rose and the world that he'd never been in love and was still waiting to fall fast and furiously in love with someone he could spend forever with?

He and Venus rode in silence, the Paris nightlife filtering into the limo as they passed by bars and restaurants lit up and busy with people lingering at outside tables.

Finally, he sat back. "Do you want me to put an end to all of this and make a statement that we're just friends and nothing more?"

"What's the point?" She released a scoffing laugh. "After the kiss we just shared, I doubt anyone would believe it."

"True." Anyone watching the kiss had to have seen

how affected he'd been. "Then at least I can tell them we have no plans to get engaged."

A text pinged on her phone. In the dark, Reed's name flashed brightly. She glanced down to read it, and Brock watched out his window to give her some privacy.

She was quiet for several beats, then snorted. "Well, that's just wonderful."

"What is?" He shifted back around.

"Reed's angry about our engagement."

"But we're not engaged."

"Apparently, there's a picture of you leaving Tiffany's with a tiny bag in hand, and it's splashed all over social media."

9

Venus read Reed's texts again.

> **Reed:** *Are you crazy?*
>
> **Reed:** *I can't believe you're even considering getting engaged to Brock.*
>
> **Reed:** *Are you doing this because I told you that you're afraid of committing?*

"It had to be my manager." Brock pulled out his phone. "He must have planted the photographer at Tiffany's."

She wanted to shoot a text back to Reed and tell him she wasn't engaged and that he was wrong. They'd always had the kind of friendship where she could be honest with him about everything. She wasn't used to holding back and deceiving him.

But she'd started the whole fake dating because of him. Not only had she needed to prove to him she wasn't like her mom and afraid of commitment, but maybe in some ways, she wanted to force herself to move on, show him what he was missing in giving her up, and make him regret not choosing her.

Brock started typing out a text on his phone. "I'll text Harper and ask him to come up with a plan to get rid of this whole engagement thing."

"Wait."

He paused and glanced at her.

Her mind was a tumble of confusion. She'd assumed she could pair herself with Brock in theory for a couple of weeks or maybe a month and then move on easily. But already, after just one week, the situation was beginning to spiral out of control.

Brock reached for her hand on the seat between them. He squeezed it gently before letting go.

The move only made her think about his hands, which had been on her a few minutes ago when they'd kissed outside Maxim's. His fingers had splayed at her back, pressing her tighter as he'd meshed his mouth with hers. And oh, what a meshing it had been.

A sizzling started again in her stomach, just as it had when she'd been kissing him—a sizzling like that of a sparkler all lit up and hissing and spitting out tiny flickers. She hadn't been prepared for those mini fireworks going off inside her. Brock McQuaid was not only the king of country music. He was obviously the king of kissing too. He'd kissed her back with a decisiveness and a banked passion that had been both hot and exciting.

She was embarrassed to admit she hadn't been ready for the kiss to end when it did. If she'd had her way, she might have kissed him longer—although that only would have added to the rumors about them.

Were the rumors really all that bad? They weren't harming anyone or anything. "Maybe it wouldn't hurt to let Reed think I'm engaged."

Brock set his phone on his leg. "Do you think an engagement will make him jealous?"

"He really does love Lexi. But maybe if I'm getting serious, it will make him start to see me as a woman and not just a friend." Was that what she really wanted now after hearing how much he loved Lexi?

"In other words, you want him to see you as a marriageable option before he rules you out and goes through with marrying Lexi."

"Yes. No. Maybe. I don't know."

"Wow. That's super clear."

She couldn't hold back a laugh.

He chuckled too.

"I'm sorry I'm making this so complicated."

"I don't mind. Like I told you, I'm here for whatever you need. And if you want a fake fiancé instead of a fake boyfriend, I can do that."

She settled her hand on top of his where he'd crossed it over his bicep. "Thank you, Brock. You've been great about everything. I couldn't ask for a better fake boyfriend or fake fiancé."

"You're welcome."

Although she couldn't see his grin, she could sense it in his words. "We're technically not engaged yet. You've only bought my ring."

"And technically, I haven't done that either."

She gave him a playful shove, then let go of his hand. "We'll let everyone assume that's what you were doing at Tiffany's without confirming or denying the rumors. Eventually, everyone will forget about it."

"You don't think they'll expect a grand proposal?"

"Not if we don't bring it up."

"If I were going to propose to you, you'd better believe I wouldn't do it at a lame party."

"Reed's party wasn't lame."

"I'd make sure it was a surprise, and I'd do it somewhere meaningful."

"Reed's always been more practical and sensible, just like me. That's one reason why we've always gotten along so well."

"By practical you mean predictable and boring?"

She pushed his arm again. "As opposed to spontaneous and reckless?"

"The way I see it, I get enough spontaneity and

recklessness on my own without having someone else to make things worse. What I could really use is a person to balance me out."

"Oh, so you need my predictability and boringness? Is that what you're saying, my almost fake fiancé?"

"Maybe that's the blessing of marriage," he said with a sincerity that surprised her. "That two imperfect people come together and are able to help each other in their weaknesses."

The more time she spent with Brock, the more she realized she hadn't really known him, that he was deeper and more insightful than a lot of people she knew.

Their limo had come to a halt in front of their hotel, and in some ways she was a little sad their date was coming to an end. A part of her wanted to suggest going for a walk. However, she didn't want to mislead him into thinking she felt anything for him beyond their friendship. Yes, they'd kissed. And they might have to kiss again at some future date in order to continue to make their relationship believable. But it was all practical, and they couldn't let it lead to anything more.

As the chauffeur opened their door, Brock looked at her and held out a hand. "Ready to put on one last show for the evening?"

She placed her hand in his. "Of course I am. Don't forget I'm the one who kissed you first."

"Oh, believe me"—his voice turned to a low growl—

"I won't be forgetting that kiss."

Something in his tone sent delicious tingles up her spine. As she allowed him to assist her from the limo into the well-lit hotel entrance, he intertwined their fingers and gave her a smoldering look that brought the sizzling sparklers back to life in her stomach.

Was this all for show? Or was any of it real?

She glanced around at the few guests standing in the outside courtyard as well as some tourists passing by. From what she could tell, there were no paparazzi or photographers. Brock didn't need to be laying on the charm so thick. But if she was honest, she didn't really mind.

Hand in hand with Brock, she walked into the hotel lobby and then to the elevators. Once inside and with the door closed, Brock released her hand and grinned. "How'd I do, darlin'?"

"You did great." She had the urge to slip her hand back into his and rest her head against his shoulder. She had the feeling he would be a strong person to lean on, that he'd be there and hold her up no matter what she was going through. Reed had once been that person for her. But when was the last time he'd really been there for her?

Yes, they'd kept in contact and remained friends, but if she was honest, there had been a shifting apart, visiting less often and not sharing as deeply. She couldn't pinpoint when that distance had started. It had probably been gradual for both of them. Not to mention that he had Lexi and didn't need anyone else in the same way.

Now, with Brock by her side, the distance with Reed seemed even greater and left her feeling emptier. As tempting as it was to open up to Brock and let him into her life, the trouble was that Brock was only filling in. All that they had was based on a lie. It wasn't permanent. And she couldn't forget that.

After four days in Cannes for her photo shoot for Fitzsimmons, she flew to Berlin. Even though she'd tried to get out of going to Brock's concert there, he'd already made arrangements with his manager to have her come.

His assistant, Ella Mae, met her at a side door of the Uber Arena and led her through a maze of hallways.

Venus had dressed more casually for the concert, in vintage Levi's, knee-high brown boots, and a brown leather jacket over a white eyelet crop top. She'd left her hair down and had parted it in the middle and straightened it.

"He's already taken the stage." Ella Mae's high ponytail swished with each step she took. She wore an oversized T-shirt with Brock's logo, simple black leggings, and high-top Converse.

Venus had met Ella Mae previously but had never really interacted with her. Now, as she followed after the young woman, she couldn't stop a twinge of jealousy from surfacing. Why? Venus didn't understand it. Because Ella Mae had access to Brock all the time? Was in charge of his schedule? Knew everything about him, so much so that she picked out his clothing every day?

"He's been looking forward to your visit." Ella Mae tossed her a smile over her shoulder.

"He has?" Ella Mae knew the relationship with Brock was fake, didn't she?

"For the past hour, all he's done is ask if you're here yet."

"Really?" Why did that bit of information make Venus's heart patter faster?

"He'll be glad to see you."

Venus wanted to deny that she would be glad to see him too. But she couldn't. During her flight there, she'd flipped through the pictures on social media of him at his concert earlier in the week in Reykjavík. There were a few photos of him on stage in faded jeans, scuffed cowboy boots, and a tight black T-shirt that showed off all his muscles. She'd come across some pictures of him greeting fans, his crooked smile in place. Then there had been one of him entering a hotel alone.

No more playing around for Brock McQuaid. Does this mean the hottest country music star has really given his heart away to just one lady? The post had gone on to say that he'd last been seen with her in Paris and no other women since. The article had also mentioned the rumors about him purchasing an engagement ring but speculated that was only hearsay and it was probably too soon for the world's most eligible bachelor to be thinking about settling down.

The first day or two in Cannes, Venus had faced questions about the supposed ring purchase. She just shrugged her shoulders and answered vaguely with lines like "If he has, he's keeping it a surprise."

She'd answered Reed's text with the same reasoning. He'd proceeded to caution her not to rush into anything, and she'd been snarky back. *Oh, like you?*

They'd only exchanged a few texts since, mostly details for his wedding.

She'd thought about sending him another text today and apologizing for getting angry and being abrupt. But she was hoping to see him next week in New York City and had decided she could try to make peace with him then.

Ella Mae picked up her pace. "We're almost there."

The music had grown louder with each turn of a corner. Ahead, security stood with arms braced at the foot of a set of metal stairs that led to a curtained-off stage. People clustered around, most wearing lanyards. Were they press? Fans with backstage passes? Or perhaps some of his employees?

Whatever the case, they moved aside for Ella Mae, and as they took in Venus, their eyes widened.

The security officer nodded at Ella Mae and unhooked a cord to let them pass.

Ella Mae started up the steps, but Venus didn't move. She'd been backstage before for Reed's concerts and knew what to expect and how things operated. But it felt strange to be walking up to watch Brock from such a personal area.

At the top, Ella Mae halted. "You coming?"

"Maybe I should watch from the arena."

"Brock would chew me out if I let you do that."

Venus hesitated. As far as everyone else was concerned, she belonged right here, as close to Brock as possible. Besides, if he wanted her there, then she couldn't refuse him.

She hurried after Ella Mae. They passed beyond the curtain, and the stage came into view, where even more people were congregated to the side and out of sight of the audience—more band members, sound technicians, and arena crew.

Once again, the workers stepped aside at the sight of her and Ella Mae, until at last they were standing along the front row of onlookers, with a perfect view of Brock and the band behind him. He was in the middle of rapid finger work on the strings, moving expertly and swiftly.

The crowd was going wild, cheering and screaming and encouraging him on.

When he finished and glanced up with one of his happy grins, the crowd gave a deafening roar. With his easy smiles and handsome charm, it was obvious why he was one of country music fans' favorite performers and why his shows drew more people than Reed's and sold out within minutes of tickets going on sale.

In the next instant, Brock launched into the words of a song, his gritty voice ringing out and making him all the more enticing.

If he'd been having trouble with fans, they'd forgotten all about his breakup with Ainsley Rose. Or maybe they'd forgiven him, and it no longer mattered. Either way, Brock wouldn't need to be in a fake relationship with her for much longer before his reputation was restored. It was possible their relationship had already put him back on solid ground. It was even possible he'd never needed it.

As he played and sang the last half of the song, she found herself being drawn in by his charisma too. He was an easy guy to like. At least for as long as their relationship lasted, she wanted to just enjoy their time together as friends. She could let herself do that, couldn't she?

At the last note of the song, his gaze darted to the side stage and landed on her. His eyes seemed to light up more, and that cocky smile of his slipped into place.

She smiled back and gave a tiny wave.

He winked at her. Then he was facing the crowd again, talking to them over the clapping and cheering.

"He likes you." Ella Mae leaned in so that the words echoed in Venus's ears.

"I like him too."

"No." Ella Mae moved closer so that their conversation was private. "He really likes you. More than I've seen him like any other woman."

A flutter of soft wings took to flight in Venus's stomach. But she pressed her hand there to keep them from rising too high. She was here for her weekly date with Brock. That's all this would be.

10

"Hey, darlin'." Brock wrapped Venus up in a hug—the hug he'd been secretly dying to give her from the moment she'd shown up on the side stage. Somehow her presence there had charged him, giving him an extra boost of energy that the crowd had clearly felt, if their encore was any indication.

She felt as good as she looked, but he didn't linger in holding her since they were surrounded by people everywhere on the side stage—mostly band members and stage crew.

"You were great," she said as they pulled away from each other. The casual look in jeans and a brown leather coat suited her every bit as much as the fancy gown he'd seen her in for their date in Paris.

"I was showing off for you."

"You might have just made me a fan."

"Might?" He cocked a brow.

Her eyes held a playful gleam that he really liked. "Maybe a little."

"Guess I still got some work to do to win you over." As a fan? Or something more? He wasn't sure if his words had a double meaning or not.

The protection agent assigned to him by the arena nudged him, the sign that it was time to make his way to the dressing room.

He didn't ask for Venus's permission before clasping her hand in his. It would make things easier as they walked through the busy hallways. At least, that's what he was telling himself as he started to tug her along by his side.

He accepted the back slaps and teasing of his bandmates as he made his way off the stage. But he didn't stop to talk to anyone—not even Harper, who had been tracking his popularity through social media responses to his performance.

All Brock wanted to do was spend time with Venus. He was actually surprised at how intense that desire was. Maybe it was because he hadn't been able to stop thinking about her over the past week since their date in Paris. Maybe it was because people were talking about him dating Venus after more pictures had come out of them together. Maybe it was because of the engagement rumor.

Whatever the case, she'd been on his mind a lot lately,

and now that he was with her again, he was genuinely happy.

When was the last time he'd felt that way?

He couldn't remember ever being so happy when he'd been with Ainsley Rose. Actually, spending time with her had started to feel like a chore, which was another reason he'd broken things off.

As he stepped into the lounge of his dressing room with Venus, he hesitated in releasing her hand but made himself do so as Ella Mae and several other staff followed them into the suite.

He nodded toward the spread of food and drinks on a side table. "Help yourself." He crossed toward the bathroom. "It won't take me long to shower and change."

Venus didn't say anything.

He paused at the bathroom door. "You all right, darlin'?" Was she regretting that she'd come?

She picked up a strawberry from one of the platters and plucked the top off. "I lied back there on the stage."

His thrumming pulse came to an abrupt halt. It was his turn for silence.

She took a dainty bite out of the strawberry before lifting her full gaze to him. In spite of everything, her light-blue eyes knocked into him with a power that left him breathless.

"I lied about *maybe* being a fan," she said softly.

"You did?" he managed.

She nodded. "I'm already a Brock McQuaid groupie."

He snorted but was secretly thrilled with her admission.

"I have almost every one of your songs memorized."

He couldn't hold back a genuine grin. "Really?"

She grinned in response. "Really."

"Suppose now you'll be wanting my autograph."

She held out her hand, palm facing up. "Yes. Right here."

Was she being real? Or was this a show for the few staff mingling in the room?

It didn't really matter, did it? He swiped up the Sharpie Ella Mae was holding out to him from where she'd been picking an outfit for him to change into.

He crossed to Venus and stopped in front of her. Gently, he took her outstretched hand, popped off the lid on the marker, then hovered above her palm.

She cocked her head, her attention already fixed raptly on the Sharpie.

For most people, he just wrote his name. But that seemed too impersonal for Venus. So he penned the first thing that came to his mind. A heart. Then the words *It's yours*.

As soon as it was written, he closed her fingers over it and spun away from her. He tossed the marker back at Ella Mae and then crossed to the bathroom again. Feeling Venus's gaze following him, he glanced over his shoulder at her.

She had her palm open and had obviously read what he'd written. And she was smiling at him, a happy smile.

Relief swirled through him that he hadn't overstepped himself with the message. Even so, he winked and forced himself to stay nonchalant, not wanting to appear overly eager to be with her, even though he was.

A short while later, after he'd freshened up, his driver took them to the Berliner Fernsehturm for dinner. The sphere restaurant that was two hundred meters above the ground had a spectacular view of the city.

They stayed late, taking in the sights. After that, they went to the Brandenburg Gate, lit up at night, then to Berliner Dom cathedral, where Harper had somehow managed to get them a private tour guide who took them up into the dome for another look at Berlin from up high.

They found a twenty-four-hour diner and ordered coffee and strudel. By that time, the night was already well on its way to being over. So Brock convinced Venus to stay up the rest of it and go with him to the sprawling garden at the city center. They walked the quiet paths for a while before reclining in the thick grass near one of the ponds.

Brock wasn't ready for his time with Venus to come to an end, but the night was quickly fading, and the first hints of morning would soon touch the edges of the lush foliage of the Tiergarten.

From the corner of his eye, he could see Ella Mae by

the light of a park lamppost down the path, motioning that it was time to go, that Venus had to leave to catch her flight.

"I can't believe I let you convince me to stay up all night." Venus was stretched out on her back.

He was resting his head on his bent arm. "It was every bit as much fun as I predicted, wasn't it?"

"Arrogant much?"

"Admit it," he persisted. "You loved our whirlwind tour of Berlin."

"Fine. Maybe." She stifled a yawn behind her hand.

He rolled to his side and gently poked her in the ribs.

She startled, then laughed.

He leaned closer and this time tickled her more.

She wiggled back, laughing again.

"You loved it." He could easily concede that he'd loved every second of their time together, and he wished she could go with him to Dublin and his concert in London next week as he ended his tour. But she'd shared about all the different companies that she was modeling for over the next week, and she had hardly a free minute to spare.

With her laughter filling the early morning, she pushed up to her feet and away from his fingers, more relaxed and at ease than he'd ever seen her. She'd used a big clip to put her hair up into a messy bun, but somehow even the mess was beautiful, and he could only stare at her with an adoration that had been growing all night.

Yes, she was incredibly beautiful on the outside, but she was also spirited and interesting and witty and smart and kind and more. In fact, the list was growing too long to contain everything he liked about her. While he'd already known some of those qualities about her, he'd only gotten glimpses of them previously. Now, after spending concentrated time together, she seemed to be letting him see everything about her.

Her laughter faded, and she tucked back a strand of loose hair. "What's wrong? Do I have something in my hair?"

"Nothing's wrong." He didn't move. Instead, he wanted to capture this moment. Standing in the last of the moonlight, her hair the pale gold of a dream, her skin the soft silk of cream. And all he wanted to do was look at her for a forever night.

For a forever night.

The lyrics spun through his head, and the melody hummed in his blood. He'd written another song over the past week, inspired by their time in Paris. Now this new song was swelling inside him and demanding that he write it and play it.

"You're staring at me," she whispered.

"Can't help myself." He propped up on his elbow.

"Don't say it." She fisted a hand on her hip.

"Say what?"

"That you think I'm beautiful or something like that." Her tone was exasperated, as if she was tired of such compliments.

"That wasn't what I was gonna say."

"Then what?"

He wasn't sure he wanted to tell her the truth. It was a little embarrassing.

"That was it, and now you can't think of anything else to say instead." She spun and began to walk away from him.

"Venus, wait." He scrambled up and stalked after her. He caught up with her and gently tugged her to a stop.

She pivoted around, her brows slanted and her features tight.

He had to say something. It might as well be the truth. "Seeing you in the moonlight. It made me think of the lyrics for a new song."

Her eyes widened. "Really? That's what you were thinking?"

"It's the honest truth." Since he'd already started, he may as well tell her everything. "Ever since we started talking at Reed's engagement party, I've been back to writing some songs."

"You're back? Does that mean you were having trouble?"

"Yep." He stared down and toed his boot in the grass.

"I've had writer's block for a while and was starting to lose hope that I'd have any songs by the time my album's due."

"Oh."

He palmed the back of his neck. That wasn't the response he'd hoped for. But now that he'd told her the truth, there was no taking it back.

She was quiet for several more heartbeats. "So you're saying I'm your inspiration?"

Was she? "Guess I didn't think of it like that. But maybe you are."

The tension in her shoulders seemed to ease. "I'm going to take credit for your new burst of inspiration."

"Is that right?"

"Yes. In fact, I deserve a cut of profit from your next hit."

"I'll be sure to send you a check."

"Good." The lines in her face had smoothed out, the frustration now gone.

He reached up and caressed her cheek.

She stopped breathing.

"Listen, darlin'." He wasn't sure why he'd touched her cheek. He dropped his hand away and took a step back. "I'm trying not to focus on how you look, because there's so much more to you than your beauty."

She was watching him intently.

"But if I want to admire how pretty you are once in a

while, can you let me do it without getting mad?"

"Maybe." She tilted her head and seemed to be trying to see deep inside him.

He was usually open and honest about most things. Of course, he'd had to hide the truth about this fake relationship with Venus from everyone. But sometimes— like over the past night—their relationship didn't feel so fake anymore. It felt real, his attraction felt genuine, and he didn't feel like he was pretending. Like now.

"Will you let me admire how good-looking you are, then, too?" Her voice took on a teasing quality that he liked.

"Darlin', you can admire me all you want. I won't object."

She laughed lightly. "It is hard to stop admiring you, but I'll force myself."

He expelled a full breath. At the same time, he caught sight of Ella Mae waving at him more urgently. "Hate to put an end to all your admiring, but Ella Mae's about to come over and drag us to the car if we don't hurry on up."

He rode with Venus to the airport. At the drop-off area, he helped her out and didn't let go of her hand. Instead, he tugged her into a hug.

"I don't see any paparazzi or reporters," she whispered against his neck as she slid her arms around him. There were other passengers being dropped off, but no one seemed to be paying them any attention at the predawn hour. "I think we're okay if we don't kiss goodbye."

He hadn't expected a kiss, but now that she'd mentioned one, the desire to taste her lips rose up swiftly, and the memories from their kiss in Paris came rushing back. "Maybe we should kiss…just in case." He made sure to infuse enough teasing into his tone that she wouldn't take him seriously.

She pushed against him playfully. "What? Do you need more inspiration?"

"Yep, and a kiss would help a whole lot."

She was smiling up at him, her eyes alight with happiness.

Was it possible that he was the cause of her happiness? That he was the one putting that light in her eyes? Either way, whether he was or not, he wanted to be the one to make her happy, to make her smile and laugh, to make her look up at him with radiant eyes. He wanted to go on doing it for the rest of his life, and he couldn't imagine anything else that would ever matter as much.

A quick and sharp pressure clamped his chest, snagging his breath. What was going on with him? Why was he thinking like this about Venus? His feelings were too intense and were pumping through him too fast, too furiously.

Fast. Furious. Just like in the McQuaid legacy of love that happened to McQuaid men when they found the woman they were passionate about.

That couldn't be happening to him. Not with Venus. Not when she was in love with and wanted to marry another man.

Brock took a rapid step back, the vise around his chest rising and threatening to strangle him.

Her smile faltered. "Is everything okay?"

He forced a quick smile and cleared his throat, trying to dislodge the tightness in his throat. "Everything's fine. Sad to see you leaving, that's all."

It wasn't all. But he'd already said enough at the park about how she was becoming the inspiration for his songs. He couldn't say anything else. Besides, it wasn't true that he was falling for Venus with the same passion other McQuaid men had fallen for their women. He wouldn't let it be true.

He certainly wouldn't tell her. It would scare her away forever, and he wasn't ready for that to happen.

She glanced down at her phone. "I suppose we could exchange phone numbers."

"Probably a good idea. Since we're practically engaged and all."

She took his phone and typed in her contact information, then handed it back to him. "Send me a message."

He typed in a few short words and hit Send.

She didn't read the message and instead took hold of

the handle of her suitcase, which their driver had placed beside her. She twisted it and seemed to be stalling, almost as if she wanted to say something more. Then she smiled at him again, but this time it wasn't genuine. He wasn't sure how he could tell, he just could.

"I hope your last concerts go well."

He couldn't let her leave without making her smile again for real. "They won't go as well as last night's concert, but without you here, darlin', what do you expect?"

Her eyes lit up again.

He breathed out a tight breath he hadn't known he was holding.

She turned and began to walk away, rolling her suitcase alongside her. She cast him a final glance. "I'll be expecting to hear the new song from the park when I see you next."

"Is that right?"

"No excuses."

He chuckled.

A moment later, she crossed through the sliding glass doors. She was elegant and graceful with just a hint of seduction to her sway. He wanted her to turn back around and give him one last smile. But she kept going and disappeared around a corner. Even then, he waited, hoping for one last look at her.

At the honk of a car in the drop-off lane, he tore his

gaze away. Only then did he realize how hard his heart was pounding and how tense his muscles were. With need for her, a need that he hadn't realized had been building inside him but that now couldn't be contained. He didn't want to drive away from her, didn't want to be apart from her for even a minute.

In fact, his body keened with such longing to be with her that he was tempted to chase after her and pull her into another hug and this time kiss her. The desire swirled with a strength that left him breathless again.

He'd never felt this way about any woman, as if he'd be empty and useless and nothing else in his life had mattered until he'd met her.

He took a step toward the door, then stopped himself.

No, he couldn't go after her. What they had wasn't real. The feelings between them weren't real. And a future with her wasn't real.

He couldn't let himself think that it was.

# 11

She hadn't heard from Brock in five days.

Venus glanced at the text he'd sent her at the Berlin airport the morning they'd exchanged phone numbers.

Brock: *I'll miss you.*

If he'd planned on missing her, why hadn't he texted her?

She flipped her phone over onto the bistro table and sat back in her chair, examining the faded heart and words Brock had written on her palm. They were almost gone now. But she couldn't deny that she'd tried to keep them there as long as possible all week.

It had been sappy to do so. But she hadn't been able to stop herself.

She traced the heart as she'd already done more times than she wanted to admit. As she did so, Reed stepped inside the brightly lit restaurant, combed his fingers through his sandy-blond hair, then glanced around. As his gaze landed on her already sitting at a table, he started forward through the maze of ferns and bamboo decorations.

She smiled and waved, waiting for the usual rush of feelings to surface—the admiration for his good looks, the happiness of seeing him again after the weeks apart, and the longing to make their relationship more serious.

But even as she willed herself to be excited to have lunch with him, the ring of an incoming text distracted her, and she quickly turned her phone back over.

It was just from Kristin, confirming that she had canceled the last appointments for next week—the vacation week of the fake relationship with Brock. Venus had expected Brock to at least ask her where she wanted to go, but apparently neither Brock nor his people had anything lined up yet.

Maybe he'd changed his mind about taking a vacation with her, and maybe she'd just take the week off to go home to the ranch in Malibu.

Whatever the case, she was glad to spend some time with Reed while he made a quick stopover in New York before flying to Nashville for some publicity stuff.

"Hey," he said as he neared the table. Unlike Brock, who wore his jeans and boots and cowboy hat because of the ranching lifestyle he'd grown up with, Reed only wore the country attire when he absolutely had to. Most of the time he wore joggers and a long-sleeved tee like he was doing today.

She stood and embraced him. As his arms surrounded her, she closed her eyes and breathed him in, the woodsy spice of the Dior Sauvage Elixir she'd given him for his last birthday. Some of the comfort and warmth of his presence began to penetrate the irritation she'd been harboring toward him.

He pulled back and swept his gaze over her like he usually did.

With her hair pulled back in a sleek ponytail, she was attired in one of the outfits she'd modeled that morning—capris, a cropped bomber jacket, and mules. She hadn't wanted to dress up too much for Reed and make a big deal out of their lunch, because it wasn't a big deal, was it? They were simply two friends who'd had a misunderstanding and needed to get their friendship back on solid ground.

At least Reed had continued to text her once in a while, even if most of the texts had been in reaction to some of the pictures that had come out regarding her night in Berlin with Brock. She hadn't noticed any photographers following them around, but in all the pictures she'd appeared very intimate with Brock, their heads bent close together at the sphere restaurant, lying together on the blanket in the park at an angle that made them look like they were kissing. Then there was one at the airport of them hugging goodbye.

Someone on his team had arranged for the pictures to be taken and leaked them to the press, including the one of him watching her walk away at the airport, his hands stuffed in his pockets, his shoulders slumped, and his expression filled with obvious longing.

When she'd first come across that particular picture and all the comments about him being in love with her, she'd been surprised and even slightly thrilled that he'd been sad to see her go, which made his lack of communication with her all the more confusing.

"You look incredible." Reed spoke the words he always did in greeting.

Why didn't she ever get mad at Reed for focusing on her physical appearance? Was it because they were friends first and because he'd known her before she'd grown so popular? Maybe because even though he acknowledged her looks, he'd never displayed any attraction to her. And she had tried hard over recent months to attract him and had wanted him to notice her in a new way.

The trouble was, his greeting was no different than it had always been, and his words seemed unoriginal, even trite, compared to the compliments Brock had given her. She hadn't been able to stop thinking about his last one in the park, where he'd reluctantly admitted she was his inspiration for the new songs he'd been creating. She'd also appreciated his honesty when he'd asked her not to get mad at him for complimenting her beauty once in a while. To be fair to him, he'd been better than most men and hadn't been starry-eyed every time he looked at her.

Maybe there was a secret part of her that wished he had been more enamored, enough that he would want to talk with her again, at least via texts.

She returned to her seat at the table, and Reed took the spot across from her. They made small talk while they ordered, mainly discussing the wedding, which was only about five weeks away, in early October. Apparently the wedding planner had already made significant strides in getting everything organized. It was turning out to be a big event, and Reed's family was paying for everything and wasn't sparing any expense.

Venus hadn't wanted to spend the entire meal discussing the wedding, but it seemed to keep Reed from commenting on her and Brock's relationship and causing more tension.

Reed wiped his mouth on his napkin before tossing it on his empty plate. "I was thinking we could have a weekend bachelor party in Los Cabos."

"Have fun with that." She'd only eaten half of her Mediterranean salad, had learned to eat light so that she wasn't bloated during photo shoots, and now she set down her fork and took a sip of her seltzer water.

"You're coming, aren't you?" Reed's brows arched.

"I don't know—"

"You're my best woman and have to be there."

"My schedule is pretty full." She couldn't imagine spending an entire weekend helping Reed celebrate getting married to another woman. The short time at the engagement party had been bad enough.

"It's in three weeks. Kristin has plenty of time to rearrange your appearances so you can come."

She tried not to sigh. Reed knew how things worked too well and that Kristin was good at freeing up the schedule when necessary. "You go on and celebrate with all your friends—"

"I can't celebrate without you there." Reed almost sounded offended that she wasn't eager to hang out with him and some of his closest guy friends.

"Are you inviting Brock?" The question fell out before she could stop it. She supposed the conversation about him was inevitable, and she may as well get it over with.

Reed fidgeted with his spoon. "I wasn't planning on it. We're not that close anymore."

"That's not true. You invited him to your engagement party."

"That was before...before...he took an interest in you."

As with other times, she was tempted to blurt out that her relationship with Brock was only pretend. Doing so would ease Reed's mind. But a part of her was embarrassed to admit to Reed that she'd been angry and hurt over his engagement and so had agreed to fake date Brock. Doing so had been childish, but at the time of the engagement party, she hadn't known how to handle her feelings.

"You can't ruin your relationship with Brock. You need his endorsement."

"I'm doing fine." Reed's answer was sharp. "And I don't care if my friendship with him is ruined."

"That's not true."

"He's shown me his true colors with you."

"How so?"

"After seeing the pictures of the two of you in Berlin, I texted him and told him for the sake of our friendship to please break things off with you."

"You didn't."

Reed had the grace to look chagrined, but only for a moment before his brow furrowed over flashing eyes.

"What was his response?"

"He said he's not breaking things off."

She couldn't keep a strange sense of relief from pulsing through her.

"It's obvious you've fallen for his charm and that you aren't seeing who he is."

"And who, exactly, is he?"

"I told you he's a player. He'll string you along for a little while with his charm, then cast you aside once he no longer has a need for you."

Her retort stuck in her throat. Was that what had happened this week and why he hadn't texted her? Had she fallen for his charm only to have him cast her aside? Maybe he was already interested in another woman. If he could lie about being in a relationship with her, what was to prevent him from lying about other relationships?

Reed leaned forward, reached across the table, and grasped both of her hands. "I can see from your expression that you know exactly what I'm talking about."

If she'd fallen for Brock's charm, then it was her fault. They had an arrangement to pretend to date. That's all. Brock wasn't stringing her along. He wasn't casting her aside. And if he had an interest in other women, who was she to stop him? Especially when she was interested in Reed.

She patted Reed's hands. "Don't worry. Brock and I are getting along just fine."

"Come on, Venus." Reed pulled his hands away and crossed his arms. "I know you better than this. And I know there's something off between you and Brock."

"We're better than fine. We're fabulous."

Reed scoffed. "If you refuse to listen to me, then don't come crying when he breaks your heart."

"So your friendship is now conditional?"

His face fell. "Of course not. I care about you and don't want you to get hurt."

"He won't hurt me."

"You can't be sure of that."

"Please believe me, Reed." How could Brock hurt her when he'd never made any promises and their relationship wasn't real?

Reed held her gaze for a moment, then sighed. "To be honest, it's just hard to see you with one of my friends."

"Who did you expect to see me with?"

"I don't know. Maybe I'd be jealous of any guy you're with because that means you're not mine anymore."

Jealous? Because she wasn't his? She opened her mouth to respond but couldn't find the words. What did he mean?

He smiled softly. "I'm sorry. That sounds crazy."

"No, you're fine." What exactly had he meant?

"Forget I said anything. Of course you're not mine. And I have no right to be jealous."

"It's okay." Maybe his feelings ran deeper than she'd realized. Maybe he had liked her as more than a friend but had never been able to express it.

"I guess seeing you with Brock is bringing out the worst in me."

A part of her wanted to bait him to say more, to admit that he cared about her, to tell him he'd made a mistake in choosing Lexi. But another part of her knew that doing so wouldn't be right, that she couldn't influence him against Lexi. After all, she didn't want Reed to choose her by default.

"It's just that you've never dated anyone seriously. You've always been there for me, and now I have to share you."

Guilt pricked her. What would he say when he realized he wasn't really sharing her with Brock, that the whole thing was a scam?

His eyes were tender and raw and filled with something she'd never seen there before. Was it love?

Her heart sputtered. It couldn't be love. Not now. Not after he'd chosen Lexi. Not after he'd already gotten engaged. Not after he had the majority of the wedding planned and paid for.

What if her fake relationship with Brock had finally gotten through to Reed and made him realize there was more to their relationship than friendship?

Maybe fake dating Brock was working after all.

"I have to share you too," she offered.

"I know." His response was soft and sad.

She wanted to take hope in their conversation that maybe he still had room in his heart for her. But did she want him to have room? She wasn't sure anymore, and her indecisiveness surprised her more than anything.

"I tell you what," he said as he pushed back from the table. "I'll invite Brock to the bachelor party. Will that entice you to come?"

Having Brock there would make the weekend more bearable. "As long as you promise to behave toward him."

"I can't promise. But I'll try." Reed didn't bother hiding the jealousy in his tone this time.

She didn't know where that jealousy would lead, but it was there. And that was something.

12

"Brock McQuaid is finally in love!" Kade shouted as he stepped into the house.

"Hush up." Brock took a playful swing at his youngest brother and punched him in the shoulder. "Thought I told you to be quiet about it."

Kade grinned as he set Brock's bag on the back entryway floor. "You might have told me to be quiet, but I never agreed to it."

At twenty-three, Kade was the baby of the five McQuaid siblings. Brock could admit he was probably the best-looking of their bunch. As the head wrangler for Healing Springs Ranch, he spent most of his time working with horses and cattle. In his spare time, he was a bull rider. He'd gotten good enough to ride the rodeo circuit last year but had opted out of the upcoming circuit because of their dad's pancreatic cancer battle.

Kade shared the same dark hair and eyes as Brock and

a brawny body that was all muscle. But he was slightly taller than the rest of the McQuaid men. His face was narrower and his features more boyish—less rugged—with even more charm than Brock's. He attracted women everywhere he went and had a new girlfriend, a young local woman, but according to Kade, it wasn't anything serious.

Brock had chatted with Kade during the helicopter ride from the airport in Colorado Springs up to Healing Springs Ranch, which was a short distance from the tourist town of Healing Springs.

The ranch had actually been in existence in the high-country valley well before the town. It had been built by the original Wyatt McQuaid, who'd claimed land under the Homestead Act way back in 1862. He'd come West to mine for gold but didn't have any luck and so decided to invest in cattle instead. One of his brothers had driven the cattle West, and together the two of them had created an enormous cattle industry that had lasted for decades.

In addition to ranching, the McQuaid family had ventured into the tourist industry almost from the start. Wyatt's wife had been business savvy and had run an inn near the hot springs on their land. The inn had catered to the wealthy and had started the ranch's reputation as a destination for the elite. That had continued through the generations of McQuaids along with the discovery of oil, which had helped them be able to buy up more land in the area.

Nowadays, the ranch was one of the most sought-after vacation spots in the country. The luxury homes and cabins set among the beautiful foothills and adjacent to the original hot springs drew some of the wealthiest people and celebrities. Not only were the food and activities that the ranch offered some of the best available, but the natural setting in the peaceful, mountainous area was top-notch as well. Of course, people still loved the hot spring that had been developed and expanded.

Brock loved his family and his home. The Colorado high country and the hard work had shaped him into the man he'd become. Even so, he couldn't escape the tension that mounted inside him every time he came back.

"Brock's home!" His mom rushed into the back entryway and threw her arms around him. Her wavy red hair was pulled up into a big clip similar to the one Venus had used, and she was wearing a long, flowy sundress that showed the freckles on her arms and shoulders. As usual, she was full of energy and hugged him tightly, the scent of sunshine and sage enveloping him.

As she pulled away, her pretty brown eyes and bright smile greeted him with a love that had never wavered, even though he knew he'd disappointed both her and his dad over the years with some of his choices and the wild lifestyle he'd led.

They'd raised their kids to be God-honoring and

upright with good morals and values. They'd hoped for each of their children to grow up and be the same kind of people they were—people who loved God, loved each other, and loved the land.

Even though no one said Brock was the black sheep of the family, he knew that's what they thought about him. He hadn't always kept a God-honoring and upright life. He hadn't always lived by the good morals and values they'd taught him. And he'd wandered far from home and their land.

"You look good," his mom said as she brushed her hand over the stubble on his cheek.

"So do you."

And she did. For a woman turning fifty-six, she looked younger than her years. Her birthday was tomorrow, and Emberly was planning a party to celebrate. His sister was good at planning parties, which made her role as the event coordinator at the ranch a perfect fit.

In fact, the last time Brock had been home was a month ago, when Emberly had planned Dad's birthday party. It hadn't been a big party, since Dad had just finished his first round of chemotherapy and had been in a rest week. But the whole family had been able to be there.

That had been right after he'd broken up with Ainsley Rose and before he'd gone to Reed's engagement party. Had it been almost a month since he'd caught Venus climbing up the trellis and attempting to eavesdrop on Reed and Lexi? Almost a month of fake dating her?

It had been a week since they'd met up at his concert in Berlin, and they were overdue for their next weekly date. They were actually due for their one-week vacation now that he'd finished his last concert in London a couple of days ago.

Harper and Ella Mae had been pressuring him to decide on a place to go. Ella Mae had sent him a number of possibilities that morning, but he hadn't looked at the list yet. She'd sent him another text a little while ago, saying that since he hadn't taken action, Harper had made the decision for him.

Brock didn't care where he went, and if Ella Mae and Harper wanted to figure it out, that was fine with him. They'd probably send him to Aruba or some other tropical island where the paparazzi could get lots of pictures of him with Venus.

While he would normally enjoy a week in a place like Aruba, he couldn't imagine spending a whole week with Venus anywhere, not after his reaction when he'd been saying goodbye to her at the airport in Berlin. Even now, just thinking about the strength of his attraction to her that morning and how much he'd wanted to be with her, his stomach clenched with a lingering need he didn't want to feel.

The photo of him at the airport, watching her walk

away, had unfortunately captured so much of his emotion and reaction that he'd been embarrassed to see the picture splashed across the internet with the words *Brock McQuaid is finally in love*. And of course, Kade couldn't stop teasing him about the photo and the words.

Brock had spent the past week trying to forget about the picture and his reaction to Venus. In fact, he'd been trying to forget about her altogether and put her from his mind. But that had been impossible, because every time he sat down to work on the new song that had come to him at the Berlin park, all the emotions and thoughts of her flooded him, drowning him in a need that only grew stronger and keener with every passing day.

A strange desperation had plagued him last night—a desperation to be with her, to just hear her voice or see her smile. He'd almost texted her today before leaving Nashville for Colorado Springs, but after starting a text at least half a dozen times, he'd finally deleted it and put away his phone.

Now that he was home, he'd prepared himself for his family's barrage of questions about Venus and his supposedly falling in love with her. Because, like Kade, no doubt they'd viewed the photos and headlines claiming he was finally in love. The photos, especially the one at the airport, did make him look like a lovesick puppy.

At least the naysayers had finally quieted, and the negativity that had been surfacing since his breakup with

Ainsley Rose had turned into background noise. It appeared he was no longer a fraud but was proving himself to be authentic about love after all.

While he was grateful fake dating Venus was repairing his tarnished image, the guilt had been growing the longer people believed he was truly in love with Venus.

He rolled his shoulders to ease the tension of living a lie. A part of him had even considered not flying home for Mom's birthday and instead lying low at his ranch in Tennessee. But with his dad's cancer diagnosis and not knowing how many years they had left with him, Brock didn't want to have any regrets about not spending time with his family, especially his dad.

"Where's Brock?" Dad called from the other room, his voice tinged with excitement. And sounding stronger than last month.

"How is he today?" Brock whispered.

During the ride up to Healing Springs, Kade had already filled Brock in on Dad's recent round of chemotherapy for the pancreatic cancer. Brock also kept in touch regularly with everyone, especially Kinsey, Tyler's fiancée, who was still Dad's primary nurse.

But it was one thing to get updates and another to see his dad and how weak he'd become over the past months.

"He's still pretty tired," Mom whispered back. "But he's in good spirits, especially today in knowing you're coming home."

"C'mon now!" Dad bellowed. "Let me see Brock."

Mom gave Brock a final pat.

He braced his shoulders and put on his biggest grin. Then he stepped into the large kitchen that opened up into the great room, where his dad was resting in a leather recliner. The chair was facing the wall of windows and sliding glass doors that overlooked the ranch along with the mountains to the west. The view was one of the best things about the house, although the rest of the house was decorated in all western decor and had been featured in magazines because of how unique and well-designed it was.

Brock crossed to his dad, hugged him, and pulled up a chair so that he was right beside him. Dad had lost his hair from all the chemotherapy, his face was thinner, and his body seemed frail. But his color was good, his mood happy, and his energy decent. He wanted to get up and do things for himself, but every time he so much as put a foot on the ground, Kinsey was there ordering him to take it easy and promising him that if he was careful today, she'd let him up for a while tomorrow during the birthday party.

The rest of the family came and went, a happy hub of activity. Brock's nephew Wyatt was the most excited to see him and brought out the guitar Brock had bought for him to show off all he'd learned to play over the past month. Tyler joined them and caught him up to date on all the latest ranch happenings. Emberly visited but didn't stay for long since she still had party details to finalize. The only one missing was Dustin, and he was in Russia for an executive protection agent assignment that he couldn't say anything about.

Through it all, Brock could sense his dad's eyes upon him, trying to see inside him more deeply. What was Dad hoping to find? The truth about Venus?

What was the truth? Brock didn't even know anymore. All he knew was that he was having a harder and harder time keeping his thoughts from returning to her, even against his best efforts.

After they cleared away the remains of the steak dinner Anson, their housekeeper, had made, Tyler shuttled Wyatt off for a bath, and Mom sat down in the kitchen nook to help Kinsey with wedding planning. Dad had returned to his recliner after dinner, watched the sunset, and now had his eyes closed. Brock had taken the chair next to him again.

Silence settled over the great room, and Brock leaned his head back and stared up at the high ceiling beams. Like it or not, his mind jumped immediately to Venus. Where was she tonight, and what was she doing?

Dad released an exasperated sigh. "You finally gonna tell me about this new gal of yours?"

Brock didn't move except to crack a grin. "That took you long enough."

"Reckoned you'd say something by now."

"Reckoned you'd bring it up by now."

His dad chuckled.

Brock sat forward. He hadn't wanted to talk about Venus with his dad, but he'd also known he wouldn't be able to avoid the conversation forever. He'd already gotten some teasing about her, but he'd batted away most of the pitches thrown his way without having to say much.

He couldn't do that with Dad. He'd have to say more. The question was, how much more? And the second question was like it—how much should he reveal about his arrangement with Venus? Should he at the very least confess that the relationship had been set up by their managers in order to help them both?

Doing so would cement his role as the bad boy of the family. He'd lose any remaining respect Dad might still have for him, and he'd prove he didn't have what it took to join the ranks of strong McQuaid men who had been a part of the legacy of love.

On the other hand, what would it matter if he continued the charade? He and Venus had made it through one month together. They only had two more to go, and during those two months, he'd make sure he kept things lighter to prevent his feelings and attraction from getting tangled up.

His family wouldn't ever meet Venus or see him with

her. They could assume whatever they wanted, including that he was in love with her. In the end, it wouldn't matter. He and Venus would go their separate ways, and his family would believe he'd failed at another relationship.

Because that's what he was good at—failing at meaningful relationships.

"So," his dad started again. "Are the news reports true? Do you love this woman?"

Brock hesitated. Even if he tried to deceive his dad, he wasn't sure he could. His dad had always been incredibly perceptive, seeing past the walls to the truth.

His dad sat forward, his expression suddenly earnest. "You do."

"I didn't say that."

"I could tell from the photo I saw."

Brock pushed up from his chair, strode toward the wall of glass, and then stopped and stared out. The darkness of the night prevented him from seeing much, but the moon overhead was large and bright, and even the sight of it reminded him of Venus and the new song he'd been writing.

Would everything always remind him of her?

He stuffed his hands in his pockets. The ache inside swelled swiftly, along with the need to see her again as he had that early morning with the moonlight spilling over her hair and face.

"Does she feel the same way about you?" his dad asked.

"No. Her feelings are definitely not the same." At least he could be honest about that. Whatever he was feeling toward Venus, she didn't reciprocate.

His dad was silent, probably wondering what Brock wasn't telling him—that she was in love with her best friend and wanted to marry him but couldn't because he was engaged to someone else.

"She'll get there eventually," his dad said quietly and with an assurance that did nothing to assure Brock.

"I'm not holding my breath." Venus wouldn't *get there*. She wanted to be with Reed.

Brock had never been the kind of man who went around trying to win over a woman who loved someone else, and he didn't plan to start now. The simple truth was that Venus was off-limits. She wasn't an option for him.

Dad sat forward. "All the McQuaid men have had to work hard at winning the women they love. None of the winning was easy, and at times it seemed downright impossible."

"This is beyond impossible."

"She's in a relationship with you, so there's some hope."

Brock couldn't keep from letting his shoulders slump.

"I'm not supposed to tell you this," Dad whispered.

"It's supposed to be a surprise. But she's coming tomorrow and staying here for a week."

Brock pivoted to face his dad, who was still in his recliner and was now watching Brock's expression, probably expecting to see joy or excitement or anticipation.

But Brock felt none of that. The emotion pummeling through him instead was dread. He didn't want Venus visiting the ranch for their agreed-upon one-week vacation. It was hard enough for him to be around his family and know he wasn't living up to their expectations. He certainly didn't want to be around them with Venus and have to deceive them even more.

His dad's expression remained hopeful. "If she's coming to spend a week with you, that has to be a good sign, right?"

All it meant was that Harper had gone ahead and done as he'd threatened and planned the vacation without Brock's input. What'd happened to Aruba or any of the other places on the list? Harper knew that he and Venus wanted to leave their families out of their fake relationship.

As soon as Brock was alone later, he would call Harper and tell him to change the plans and come up with a different vacation destination.

"What's wrong?" his dad persisted.

"Just because she agreed to come doesn't mean she'll

fall in love with me." In fact, his whole family might even catch on to the charade and expose him and Venus for their fake relationship. Not that his family would tell anyone or expose them for their deception. But Brock was tired of disappointing his dad. And this would be an epic fail—the biggest yet.

His dad smiled. "You'll work on wooing her all week."

"Wooing?" Brock forced a smile back. "What are we, back in olden times?"

"You know what I mean." His dad chuckled. "You'll do what we McQuaid men are good at. You'll win her over by showing her just how much you love her and want her and need her."

The protest rising inside Brock halted. If his feelings were love—and he wasn't admitting they were, not yet—then what if it was possible to win her over? Was it worth trying to use the week to *woo* her? To shower her with affection? To do everything and anything for her?

For a long moment, he let the possibility roll around inside him. Then he pressed a hand to his gut to stop the momentum.

He couldn't try anything. At least, not until he knew where she stood in relation to Reed. If she was still determined to be with Reed, then it wouldn't be right to get in the way, even though he was half tempted to do so after Reed's text this past week telling him not to get engaged to Venus. Reed's exchange had been rude, almost arrogant, and Brock had put an end to it with a quick "It's none of your business, man."

Regardless of Reed's interference, Brock didn't plan to intentionally sway Venus and then have her eventually wonder if she'd made a mistake in choosing him over Reed.

"You might have a lot of hard work ahead of you, son." His dad's voice turned grave. "But think about the other option."

"What other option?"

"The prospect of life without her in it." Dad glanced in the direction of the kitchen nook, where Mom was still sitting with Kinsey in front of a laptop screen. "I can't imagine a future without your mom. It's impossible."

Brock had always appreciated the way his dad loved his mom, as if the whole world revolved around her. Dad was tender and sweet and sacrificial, loving her unconditionally and putting her needs above his own. She blossomed in his presence because she knew she was his priority and the love of his life. In return, she loved him back just as much. It was a beautiful example of what marriage was supposed to be like.

Brock had long ago given up hope that kind of relationship would be his. As much as he longed to take his dad's advice and apply it to Venus, he didn't want to resurrect his hope only to have it crushed in the end.

Yep. Having Venus at the ranch was a bad idea. They needed to be in a place where they could keep their distance from each other but still pretend they were together.

Dad's phone dinged with an incoming text. He glanced down at his phone, then smiled warmly at Brock again. "Looks like she's already on her way."

Brock's muscles tensed. "I thought you said she was coming tomorrow."

"She was planning to get a hotel in Colorado Springs for the night, but I told her if she wanted, she could stay here tonight. We've got extra rooms."

"You've been texting Venus?"

Dad's brows rose. "Is there something wrong with that?"

Brock kneaded the back of his neck and the rising tension there. He couldn't protest, but he had to say something. "This isn't a good idea."

"It's a great idea."

"Dad, c'mon." Brock released an exasperated sigh. "I'm not ready to have you guys interfering in my relationship with her."

"Maybe it's just what you need to get things moving along."

It wasn't what he needed at all. But he was stuck, and there was nothing to do now but make the best of the situation.

13

Venus turned off the ignition of the SUV she'd rented and stared at the brightly lit home built on the mountainside. Had she made a mistake in coming to Healing Springs Ranch? Especially without talking to Brock about it?

The back door of the home swung open, and Brock stepped outside. The outdoor lights illuminated him with all his brawn and muscle. Wearing his usual faded jeans, a tight T-shirt, and boots, he looked as ruggedly handsome as always, especially as he stuffed his hands in his pockets and started toward her.

After almost a week and a half without seeing him, her stomach did a strange flip at the prospect of talking to him again. Had she missed him? Was she looking forward to being with him?

During the hour drive up from Colorado Springs, she'd wrestled with those questions and still didn't have answers. All she knew was that she wasn't dreading a week with him on his family's ranch, especially with how kind his dad had been in reaching out to her.

As Brock drew nearer, she had the sudden urge to lower the visor mirror and check her makeup. But instead, she forced herself to open the door and step down.

"Hey there, darlin'." Brock grinned at her.

"Hey." The sight of that crooked grin directed at her made her stomach do a whole series of somersaults.

At the small crowd of people gathering inside the back door of his house, she guessed his family was waiting for her to arrive as well. She wasn't sure what he'd told them about their relationship, but she suspected they didn't know it was fake. Even if they did, it wouldn't hurt to give Brock a hug.

Without waiting for him to initiate, she leaned into him and wrapped her arms around him.

He reciprocated, slipping his arms behind her and drawing her against his body.

A sense of relief flooded her. Was it because she'd been afraid his silence meant he didn't like her anymore or want to be with her? Obviously, they were hugging to put on a show for his family. But still...he wouldn't greet her so warmly if he were upset with her, would he?

She'd actually been surprised when his people had called earlier in the day and said that he wanted her to fly to his family's ranch and spend the week with him there. She'd thought they weren't involving their families, but his manager had assured her the ranch was the perfect place for the vacation, especially because of a *Rolling Stone* interview for Brock that was scheduled there in a couple of days.

Venus breathed in deeply, catching a faint woodsy scent of Brock's aftershave. The strength of his body, the thickness of his arms, and the power of his presence were just as she remembered.

After several long heartbeats, he started to pull back, but she clung to him more tightly, not ready for their embrace to end. A part of her needed this, needed him, in a way she didn't understand.

He hesitated only a moment before relaxing into her and tightening his hold. "You okay?" he asked after a few seconds.

"Your text at the airport said you'd miss me. Did you?" The words she'd been wondering all week fell out before she could stop them.

His fingers slid up her back gently, and he combed at the long strands she'd left loose. He seemed to be stalling, as if trying to figure out how to answer her.

"Never mind," she whispered, starting to pull back. "I shouldn't have asked."

His hand at her back pinned her in place. "Yep, I missed you."

She halted.

"I thought about you all the time." His whisper held a sincerity that left no doubt he meant the words.

She melted against him. Oh, she liked him. He was so sweet and considerate and nice to her, and not because he wanted her body or thought she was beautiful. No, she sensed he genuinely cared about her as a person, and there weren't many who did.

She tugged back a little, enough that she could see his face. "You didn't text me."

His grin crept out again. "Guess that means you missed me too."

"Maybe." She couldn't hold back a smile of her own.

His gaze skimmed her face before landing on her lips, as though he was considering kissing her. To put on a show for his family? Or because he wanted to kiss her?

She glanced at his mouth too. Did it really matter why he was considering the kiss? Either way, she was okay with sharing a kiss.

She lifted on her toes and pressed a kiss to his lips, one that was short but that ended up being harder and more passionate than she'd intended. Without giving him the chance to say anything or even respond to the kiss, she spun away from him toward the back seat of the SUV, where she'd stowed her luggage.

As she opened the door and reached for her suitcase, his hand landed on her hip, and he closed in behind her.

In one movement, he brushed aside her hair, then laid a soft but hot kiss at the sensitive spot where her neck and shoulder met.

A gasp slipped out, and she couldn't move—didn't want to move. She closed her eyes and waited for him to bend in again. She wanted to feel his lips against her skin, this time for longer, wanted his fingers in her hair.

But instead of another kiss, he shifted past her, took the suitcase from her hands, and lifted it out of the SUV, as if their interaction was a normal, everyday occurrence. And it should be for her too, except that she felt anything but normal. Her world felt suddenly tilted, and she was off-balance.

What was wrong with her that she was reacting so strongly to Brock? She shouldn't be, not when this was pretend.

Of course, if she was really honest with herself, she had to admit that some kind of attraction was starting to develop between them. It had been growing since that night in Berlin, but maybe she'd just been too stubborn to acknowledge it. Was that why his lack of texting her this past week had been difficult? Because she'd wanted to stay in touch? Had missed his humor? Had missed his kindness? Had missed the easy way she could be herself with him?

She pulled in a breath of night air. She had to stay composed, couldn't let him see how much his touch had ruffled her.

She closed the door of the vehicle, shouldered her carry-on bag, then faced him again.

"I didn't know you were coming until about an hour ago," he said quietly with a glance toward his family.

"Ella Mae called me about it this morning."

"She and Harper made the arrangements without consulting me." His voice had a slight edge to it.

"Oh." So he hadn't been the one to invite her to the ranch, and maybe he didn't want her here after all. "We can have our people figure out a different place."

"That's what I'm thinking."

She took a step back and rested her hand on the door handle. "I'll go stay somewhere else tonight—"

"No." He laid his hand over hers, intertwined their fingers, then drew her away from the door. "Of course you'll stay here until we can get something else lined up."

She didn't budge. "I don't want to impose."

"You're not imposing." His tone dropped. "It's just that I don't want to lie more than necessary to my family."

"That makes sense." She relaxed again. "Then let's just tell them that we're in a relationship but that we're not as serious as the media is making us out to be. It might not be the whole truth, but it's not a lie."

He hesitated. "They're all pretty nosy, and my dad is already playing matchmaker."

She laughed lightly. "He seems sweet."

"He'll have us married by the end of the week if he has his way."

"Sounds like an ambitious man."

"Real ambitious."

They fell into their easy teasing as they crossed the driveway toward the back door. When she reached the entryway, Brock made all the introductions—to his sister Emberly, to his older brother Tyler, who was engaged to Kinsey and had a son named Wyatt, and then to his youngest brother Kade, who was a charmer just like Brock.

As they moved into the house, Venus was impressed by the authentic Western style of the decorations. Real horseshoes, barrels, wheels, and other artifacts had been used to create furniture, pictures, lamps, and more. Everything coordinated with tans and browns and creams and a splash of green in the plants. The house was as beautiful inside as it was out.

Even though Brock's father T.W. had already retired to his bedroom off the great room, Brock took her in to say hi. The middle-aged man was bright-eyed and happy to meet her, and she could easily see that Brock was right about his desire to play matchmaker.

She also met his mom, Leah, who was every bit as lovely as Brock had described. Immediately, Venus sensed the deep affection Leah had for T.W., similar to what her own mom had harbored for Marco. But it was also different, and Venus wasn't sure how.

Venus had spent the past two days at her family's ranch in Malibu, hoping to have some time with her mom. But her mom had just started seeing a new guy and had been busy with him. Venus had been disappointed that her mom was jumping into another relationship and wasn't able to see her pattern of one broken relationship after another.

"He's different," her mom had said again yesterday, "and I need to give him a chance and see where this leads." How many times had her mom said that about a new boyfriend? Venus had lost count.

Maybe that was part of the reason why, when Ella Mae had called about the vacation plans, Venus had been ready to go and hadn't stopped to question anything. As much as she adored her mom, she'd wanted to get away from having to watch her being giddy like a teenage girl, all the while knowing she would be in tears six months later when the new man didn't live up to her first love.

Whatever the case, Venus could tell right from the start that she liked Leah and T.W. But it wasn't long before Kinsey said T.W. needed to get his beauty sleep.

"Don't forget the house rules, Brock," T.W. called as Venus and Brock crossed the room.

Brock stopped in the doorway and arched a brow at his dad.

T.W. leveled him a stern look. "Separate bedrooms and no hanky-panky."

"C'mon, Dad." Brock's voice was tinged with embarrassment. "Our relationship's not like that. And believe it or not, I'm not like that either."

Venus could only watch the exchange in surprise. She'd assumed Brock had engaged in his fair share of intimate relationships. Had she been wrong about country music's hottest hunk? Or was he trying to pacify his dad?

"Good." T.W. closed his eyes and leaned his head back against the hospital bed that was elevated halfway. "You know what I always say. God made man to cherish the woman for who she is and not what he can get from her."

"Yep. I know that, Dad."

Venus recognized that line from one of Brock's popular songs. Now she knew where he'd heard it, and that made it even more special.

With T.W.'s and Leah's goodnights following them, Brock led her to the great room and then out one of the sliding glass doors, where the light from inside illuminated the balcony. The cool September air greeted them along with the scent of pine and campfire smoke.

As soon as Brock closed the glass door behind them, he stalked over to the railing, bent over, and dropped his head. "Shoot. I'm real sorry about all that in there, Venus."

"Don't be." She wound her way past the patio furniture and an elaborate outdoor firepit table.

"My dad's a real stickler when it comes to how we treat women."

She wanted to brush a hand across Brock's back, but after her reaction earlier with their hug and their short kisses, she didn't want to fan any more flames. Instead, she hummed the line from his song about God making man to cherish the woman.

With his elbows braced on the railing, he peeked at her sideways. "Yep. He was my inspiration for that song."

"I always thought it was one of your best. From how popular it is, I'm guessing your fans like it too."

He ducked his head again, but a slight grin curved up his lips.

"I think I owe your dad thanks for how well he trained you."

His gaze snapped to her.

"You've treated me better in the short time I've known you than any other man has."

"Really?"

"Reed treats me well. But as you know, he's always been just a friend." At least he'd admitted at their lunch in New York last week that he was a little jealous of other men in her life. But what could come of it? Nothing when the woman he wanted to marry was Lexi.

"You deserve to be cherished by every man."

"It doesn't always work out that way."

He was silent for a beat. "Have you dated a lot?"

"A fair share, but I was never interested in anyone for long."

"Because of Reed?"

"Maybe I've never given other men a fair shot because of my feelings for him." She shrugged one shoulder. "Reed thinks it's because I can't commit."

"I guess when you care about someone, it's hard to make room to care about anyone else."

Did his statement have a hint of a question to it? Was he trying to decide whether she was willing to care about him? No, he couldn't be. She drew in another breath of the fresh mountain air. "What about you? You have quite the reputation with women."

He was still leaning on the rail, looking so casual and yet so rugged. "I admit, I've had my fair share of girlfriends over the years."

Something inside tightened at the prospect of him spending time with other women. It couldn't be jealousy, and yet she felt strangely unsettled by the idea of him treating other women to a night on the town the way he had with her in Berlin. She wanted that to be special, something he didn't do for every woman. But maybe he did since he was such a charming man.

"I meant what I said to my dad," he said as he peered out into the dark distance. "I'm not in the business of trying to get women into my bed."

"I believe you."

He again shot her a sideways glance.

The look was probing, penetrating, sending her insides into a strange tumble.

"Trouble is," he said, "I never did anything to prove the rumors wrong over the years, and so most people believe I'm a player."

"I suppose it comes with the territory."

"Suppose so. Early on, my manager and the label thought my image as a lady's man would help my sales."

"And it did."

"Yep. I had lots of fun and enjoyed all the attention. But I've never liked hookups or one-night stands."

She nodded. "I can see that about you. Even though you're easygoing and fun-loving, you have more depth than I realized."

He straightened and turned to look at her more fully. "I appreciate that assessment. Not many people see me like that."

"Then they don't know the real you."

He seemed to be studying her face, probably wondering why she was saying so much about him. Why was she? Maybe after seeing him interact with his dad, she realized there were more layers to him. And maybe she wanted to understand him better.

"Anyone special since Ainsley Rose?" She was

prying…and maybe even fishing to find out how he felt about her. "Never mind. I shouldn't have asked."

"It's all right." His grin slid up slowly.

The sight of it made her stomach tumble again. She was starting to like his grin too much. Was it even sort of addictive?

"The only woman since Ainsley Rose is you, darlin'." The words were filled with his trademark charm.

"So we're exclusive?"

"Course we are."

His statement shouldn't make her happy, but it did. She supposed on some level she'd begun to worry he'd found someone else to be interested in this past week.

Not that he'd been *interested* in her. But they were in a semblance of a relationship for now, and she didn't want him to be paying attention to other women while he was with her.

Did that mean she had to stop paying attention to Reed? It was only fair, even though Brock had been understanding about it—hadn't asked her to stop and had always supported her getting together with Reed if that's the way things worked out.

But she wasn't sure if that's what she wanted anymore. And that scared her.

"You up for another all-nighter?" Brock asked, his voice full of challenge.

"What's there to do at night here?" She let sarcasm

infuse her question even as excitement shimmered through her.

"Are you doubting me, darlin'?"

"Yes, maybe I am."

"Then let me prove you wrong."

She honestly couldn't think of anything she wanted to do more than spend another night with Brock, talking and joking and having fun. "Fine. Prove me wrong."

14

Best night ever.

Brock took a sip of the dark-roast coffee and watched the first rays of the sunrise from the hilltop behind the house. On the long, damp grass beside him, Venus drank her coffee, her eyes fixed on the eastern horizon and the majestic show unfolding.

The truth was, he'd rather stare at her than anything else, but putting the full force of his attention on her was liable to send her running as far and as fast as she could get from him. Because the full force of his attention was too intense and was only growing more intense with every passing hour.

Even if it had been the best night—even better than Berlin—maybe he'd been foolish to spend so much time with her. He should have known that doing so would only stir the craziness inside him and make him more attracted to her.

Instead of suggesting they have another all-nighter, he should have shown her to her bedroom and let her get some rest.

What had he been thinking?

He hadn't been. That was the trouble. All rational thought fled from his brain around her.

The glow of light rimming the dark pine trees and the rugged boulders all around them was like magic, slowly gaining intensity and turning the sky into a swirl of soft pink and lavender and orange.

"It's beautiful." Her whisper was breathy.

A pang shot through his gut. He wanted to hear that breathy whisper every day, every morning, and every evening, directed at him and only him.

He gulped his coffee. As much as he tried to keep his eyes on the vista ahead, his gaze shifted to her. Her body was relaxed in the oversized sweatshirt he'd bought for her from the gift shop at the hot spring pools. Her hair was loose and wavy, having finally dried after they'd tried out every one of the pools and the luxurious hot spring itself.

Before going to the pool complex, they'd taken a moonlight horse ride to one of the higher lakes. It was a ride they offered to guests, one he'd often led during his summers home from college when he'd worked on the ranch.

Once at the lake, they'd snacked on the appetizers and sipped wine that he'd brought along. Then he'd taught her how to fish, and they'd caught two fish that he'd fried up for them with the few supplies the ranch staff kept in a shed near the lake.

After that, he'd taken her to the ranch's rodeo arena, and they'd barrel raced by the light of the stadium. She was an expert rider, had excellent horsemanship, and talked fondly about the two horses she owned and boarded at her family's ranch in Malibu.

It had been the wee hours of the morning by the time they took their horses back to the barn and unsaddled and groomed them. Even doing that had been fun with her, and they'd traded horse stories from their childhoods.

By the time Kade and his staff of wranglers had been stirring in the apartments above the barn, Brock had whisked her away, driving into town for coffee from a local coffee shop and then up to see the sunrise.

She took a sip from her paper cup and then slid him a sideways glance, catching him staring.

She'd probably caught him staring at her at least two dozen times throughout the night. As hard as he was trying not to overwhelm her, he couldn't seem to stop himself. How was it that she was growing more beautiful every time he looked at her? If her eyes weren't so luminous in the dawn light, if her features weren't so natural without makeup, if her hair wasn't so long and blowing in the cool breeze...maybe then he'd be able to keep himself from looking at her so often.

"What?" she asked innocently. "Did I spill coffee?"

"Nope, you're fine." He'd kept the comments about her beauty in check so far, and he couldn't start laying on the compliments now. He had to think of something else to explain why he was staring. "I've enjoyed my night with you and don't want it to end."

Her face seemed to light up. "More than you enjoyed the night in Berlin?"

"It's a toss-up. That was one of my best nights too."

"You sure know how to show a girl a good time." She peered at the sunrise again, but something in her tone was off.

"I sure do, darlin'."

She snorted.

What was she thinking? That he made a regular habit of planning all-night dates with women? Was she a little jealous?

He allowed himself a thin sliver of hope. "Course, I've only ever had all-night dates with you."

"Oh?" Her voice rose. "Does that mean I'm the only woman you've been embarrassed to be with during the day?"

"You're jealous."

She sat up straighter. "No, I'm not."

He laughed softly. "I like it."

"Just because I'm questioning why you're taking me on dates at night and not during the day doesn't mean I'm jealous."

"Don't worry, darlin'. I've never taken a woman on an all-day date either."

She didn't respond, but a small smile played at her lips.

She'd liked his admission. Did that mean maybe she was starting to have some feelings for him too?

Ever since he'd talked with his dad about Venus, his thoughts had jumbled together, and he didn't know what to feel or think about her. Dad had said that he ought to do what McQuaid men were good at—showing her how much he loved, wanted, and needed her.

Loved. Wanted. Needed. His emotions seemed to be pointing to all three. But he'd never been in love before, so how could he tell if that was really what he was feeling? The truth was, he wasn't good at picking women—was afraid he'd get the wrong one, afraid he'd miss out on someone special, afraid he'd make a mockery of the McQuaid legacy of love.

Maybe that's why it'd been easier to keep his relationships from getting too serious. Then he didn't have to worry about ruining a family heritage.

He wasn't a strong man like the other McQuaid men. He wasn't like them in many ways at all. So what made him think he could have the legacy of love relationship with any woman?

"So," she said cautiously, "why haven't you taken a woman on an all-day date yet?"

"Because I was waiting to do it with you."

She shoved his arm. "Be serious."

He was half serious. He'd never met anyone like Venus, never wanted to be with anyone the way he did her, and never had any desire to spend beyond a few hours with anyone but her. But he couldn't say that. What could he say instead? "I don't know. Maybe I like the night dates because then I don't have to worry about our time being interrupted by anyone who recognizes us."

"We do have more privacy."

"And we get to be together without all the pressure of having to put on a show for anyone."

She took another drink of her coffee and focused on the rising sun. "I'm pretty sure your people want you to put on a show this week."

He sighed. "Yep. Probably."

"I know so. Ella Mae informed me a team from *Rolling Stone* is coming to follow us around for a day."

"What? No."

"Yes. I think she said the day after tomorrow."

Was that why Harper and Ella Mae had chosen the ranch? Because of the interview?

He pushed up from the ground and palmed the back of his neck. "We can't have *Rolling Stone* follow us around and report on us like we're a real couple."

"That's what I told her, that it would be hard to pretend for a whole day." Venus didn't move from her spot in the grass. "But apparently your people think it'll be great publicity."

"I don't care how great it is, I won't do that to you. It's too much to ask."

She fingered the plastic lid on her cup absently. "How much social media have you looked at over the past week?"

"None." At least, none after he'd seen the picture of himself saying goodbye to Venus at the airport. He hadn't wanted to see any more embarrassing pictures of himself and Venus or the comments about them, so he'd stayed clear of any and all accounts. If he was honest, he also hadn't wanted to stumble across pictures of Venus this week either. He hadn't wanted to see her gorgeous face and body splashed across the internet and be reminded that she wasn't really his.

She flipped on her phone and scrolled for a few seconds. "Those pictures of us from Berlin have gone viral and blown up the internet." She turned her screen toward him, displaying the picture of him hugging her goodbye paired with big bold print: *The country's new power couple. The king has met his queen.*

"Shoot." It was bad.

She flipped to another article with the photo of him staring after her at the airport. *If that ain't love, what is?*

He pressed his lips together to keep himself from saying anything worse. If this was what was all over the internet, no wonder his whole family had been interested in Venus, and no wonder his dad thought he was in love with her.

"'How long until McQuaid proposes? All bets are on,'" she read. Then she was quiet as she scrolled through a few more, and he was glad she didn't read any more aloud. It was downright embarrassing to have her see what everyone was saying about how much of a goner he was over her.

She finally lowered her phone, the screen going dark.

Where did he even start? He could at least apologize for dragging her into this. "I'm sorry, Venus. I didn't realize things would get so out of hand."

"It's not your fault."

"I'll call Ella Mae just as soon as possible and tell her to cancel the *Rolling Stone* interview."

"No, don't cancel." She peered at the sunrise again.

"You've already done more than enough to save my reputation and put me back in the good graces of my fans. I refuse to put you through more of this craziness." He motioned toward her phone.

"This"—she lifted her phone—"all of the attention, has actually been good for my career too."

His next line of protest died on his lips.

"My agent called yesterday and said the requests for me have quadrupled this week." She clasped her hands more securely around her cup. "In fact, yesterday she had several multimillion-dollar offers come in from all over the world."

"Is that good? Are you happy about it?"

"It's a nice boost for my career, expanding my popularity to a new audience of fans. Yours."

"Good."

"Then you don't mind if I use your fame to increase mine?"

"Course not, darlin'. If I can help you out in any way, I'll feel a whole lot better about everything."

"Are you sure?" She peeked at him sideways. "Being connected to you is going to benefit me a lot more than the other way around."

"That's not true. You rescued me from doom."

She scoffed. "I might have rescued you from the critics. But let's be honest. The negativity wouldn't have lasted long, even if you hadn't decided to have me for a fake girlfriend. Your charm would have pulled you through eventually."

"I thought part of the reason for our relationship was so that we could show Reed a thing or two." Brock hadn't brought up Reed's name yet during their time together, but he was more than a little curious to know what was going on with the two of them.

"Yes, and I thank you for that too."

Was Reed having second thoughts about marrying Lexi? Was he recognizing the treasure he'd given up?

Brock hoped not. But now that they were talking about Reed, he suddenly needed to know. "And how are things going with Reed?" He tried to make his voice sound casual and not strangled.

"We met for lunch last week."

Disappointment stabbed Brock in the stomach, hard. That wasn't what he'd wanted to hear. But what did he expect?

"Our relationship is making him think harder about what he wants."

The disappointment only twisted in his gut all the more. "So he's questioning whether he wants to marry Lexi?"

"He didn't exactly say so. But he did admit to being a little jealous." She tossed Brock a satisfied smile. "So thank you for that."

He needed to smile back and pretend he wasn't upset. But the truth was, he was worried. Brock had known the endgame was to shake Reed up, to make him realize what he'd lost in Venus. The pictures from Berlin had apparently done that. Maybe that was why Reed had texted him and told him to break up with Venus— because he wanted her for himself.

But Brock didn't want Reed to try to win Venus back…because Venus was his.

The possessiveness swelled irrationally inside him, and he had to pace away from her so that she wouldn't see the jealousy in his face.

Venus wasn't his. Not even close. So why was he thinking that way?

Because he loved her the way the photos claimed? The way his fans claimed? The way all the articles claimed? The way his dad claimed?

Even if none of those sources had noticed or reported on anything, how could he deny the thudding of his heartbeat, the almost painful intensity of his feelings that had been growing by the hour?

Was it love? And if it was, why was he trying so hard to deny it? Because he was still afraid of choosing the wrong woman? One who might still be in love with someone else?

At her touch upon his back, his spine stiffened. He hadn't heard her get up or approach.

"We can put an end to the charade now," she said softly. "I know you didn't want to be at the ranch in the first place, and now to have *Rolling Stone* following us around for a day…"

He blew out a breath, then shifted again toward the sunrise. "It's not a big deal. We'll figure it out later."

"I'll do whatever you think is best." Her face was right there in front of him, so close. All he'd have to do was bend a few inches, and he'd be able to kiss the tip of her nose.

"You know what I think is best?" He just wanted to

put everything from his mind and enjoy this moment with her.

"What?"

He smiled and then let his gaze sweep over the mountain peaks and the first rays beginning to glaze everything in shimmering gold dust. "For now, let's enjoy the sunrise and not worry about anything else."

She opened her mouth as though she might say something more, but then she nodded and peered out over the landscape. A moment later, she laid her head against his shoulder.

The swell of emotion inside rose so swiftly and powerfully that he had to close his eyes to keep tears from forming. He wasn't a man who cried often, but at that moment, the intensity of what he was feeling for her overwhelmed him in a way he'd never experienced before.

He could no longer deny the truth. He was in love with Venus Vargas. And that scared him out of his wits.

15

Venus loved the McQuaid family, especially T.W.

"Have a good day, you two," T.W. called as she followed Brock from T.W.'s bedroom.

"You too." She'd wanted to spend more time with T.W., but the crew from *Rolling Stone* had arrived early and was already waiting for them.

"Today would be a good day to you-know-what, Brock," T.W. said from a bench where he was doing physical therapy with the PT who came to the house several days a week.

Brock stumbled a step in the hallway but didn't stop.

"If you need help, you just give us a holler." T.W. continued the conversation.

Help with what? Venus wanted to prod Brock about it, but he just picked up his pace. The rest of the family was already gone, and Anson, their housekeeper, was busy elsewhere in the house.

After the big birthday party two days ago for Leah, the family had plunged back into the ranch work yesterday. Venus and Brock had started the day doing more of the ranch activities, but he'd been right that too many people recognized him everywhere he went, and it had cut into their privacy. So they'd gone back to the house and hung out with T.W. for the remainder of the day.

They only had today left at the ranch before going to Aruba tomorrow. Although she didn't want to leave the ranch, she understood the complications Brock was facing and why he'd called his manager and made the arrangements to vacation someplace else.

"Go big or go home," T.W. shouted.

Like the complication of his family thinking they were madly in love and that Brock was considering proposing to her any day. Of course, they were reading the news that had paired her and Brock together as a supercouple, one of the hottest couples—if not the hottest—out there at the moment.

The spotlight wouldn't last forever, and Kristin had told her they needed to capitalize on the popularity while it lasted. That meant when she got back from Aruba, she would be busier than ever traveling for photo shoots. She'd set aside time for Reed's bachelor party in Los Cabos, but other than that, her schedule was now full beyond capacity.

Brock halted at the island in the kitchen, blew out an exasperated breath, then faced her. "I'm sorry," he whispered.

She waved a hand. "Don't be. I'm realizing your dad is a huge romantic at heart and thinks everyone else should be." Sunshine filled the room, coming in from the skylights in the kitchen ceiling as well as through the windows, promising a cloudless, sunny day.

"Yep. That about sums it up."

All throughout Leah's party, T.W. had kept pushing Brock to be with Venus. He'd called for them to be on the same team for horseshoes, badminton, cornhole, and all the other games they'd played. He'd made sure they sat together for dinner on the deck. Later, during the bonfire, T.W. had practically pushed her onto Brock's lap.

She hadn't minded though. She'd enjoyed every moment of the party at Brock's side. She'd thought there might be awkward moments between her and Brock in their attempt to pretend to be close. But he'd handled everything with a finesse that made their relationship seem believable. So much so that by the end of the evening, she hadn't felt like she was acting at all.

She'd fallen asleep against him in front of the bonfire—since she hadn't made up the sleep from their all-nighter the previous night. She'd awoken when he'd lifted her to transport her to her room. She'd told him she could walk, but T.W. had meddled again and insisted that Brock do the right thing and finish carrying her up. He'd even gone so far as to instruct Brock to give her a goodnight kiss in the hallway and not in the bedroom.

She and Brock had laughed about it once they reached her bedroom. But he hadn't initiated a kiss in the hallway and neither had she, even though she'd felt the chemistry charging between them, especially in that moment.

Yesterday afternoon and evening, T.W. had been just as pushy, throwing her and Brock together every chance he could find. But again, his efforts hadn't bothered her. She'd found herself enjoying a low-key afternoon playing board games, watching TV, making dinner with Brock, and then having a bonfire on the deck later, just the two of them.

She finally gathered the courage to ask him more about Ainsley Rose and what had drawn him to her, what their relationship had been like, and if he missed her. He'd initially dated her because they'd both needed each other at important functions. They'd had some fun together, but Venus had been strangely satisfied to discover that he didn't miss Ainsley Rose, hardly even thought about her.

Of course, she'd had to answer his question about what she liked about Reed, explaining the start of their friendship in high school, when he'd changed to her school and she'd befriended him when he'd had no one else. In turn, he'd helped her through one of her mom's bad breakups, had listened to her, let her cry, and had kept her strong.

Her conversations with Brock reminded her of how she'd once been able to talk with Reed, except there was a constant charge in the air between her and Brock that had never been there with Reed.

Whatever the case, it was for the best that she and Brock were leaving the ranch. She didn't need to be getting any closer to his family and stirring up longing to have the healthy bonds and love that his family shared. It made her realize all the more how dysfunctional her own family had been.

Brock braced his hip against the kitchen island. "What do you think of the agenda?" He was reading a text Ella Mae had sent them both with the schedule for the day with the *Rolling Stone* team.

Venus glanced at the list, which included a number of things like riding, hiking, and doing the ropes course. In addition, the team wanted shots of them at the house, hot spring, and the barn. They also wanted pictures of Brock with his guitar.

"The day doesn't seem too terrible." She zipped up her slim-fitting jacket that she'd paired with high-rise leggings.

"Too terrible?" Brock's brow furrowed as he started texting. "I'm putting an end to this."

"No." She grabbed his phone from his hand.

His eyes rounded, but he didn't move.

"I told you I'm willing," she insisted.

"But I don't want you dreading the day."

"I'm not. Don't forget, I'm used to being followed around by a camera and having my picture taken."

"You don't need more of that kind of pressure." He reached for his phone. "I'm canceling."

She took a step back and held it up so that he couldn't retrieve it. "We can't."

"I can and I will." He followed her and stretched after the phone.

She hopped up onto the island so that she was sitting on the edge and then lifted his phone high above her head. "What happened to the everything-is-fun Brock, the one willing to have adventures and do anything?"

"He's not willing to have adventures that make you uncomfortable."

"I won't be."

With narrowing eyes, he assessed her and the phone above her head. Then before she could react, he lunged, leaning against her and grabbing her arm all in one motion.

She squealed and tried to scramble backward, but he snaked his other arm around her middle and held her in place.

His hold was firm but gentle at the same time, and

everywhere her body intersected with his, heat cascaded over her skin. It was more than just heat. It was heat with a hum of excitement and desire. It was unlike anything she'd ever felt before with any other man, even Reed. It felt delicious and yet forbidden at the same time.

With the beginning of his killer grin tipping up the corners of his mouth, he was more than overwhelming. He was demolishing her resistance to him. "My phone, darlin'." He tugged at her arm in an effort to draw her hand down.

She resisted and jutted her chin, telling herself she was just teasing him, but at the same time, she knew she was playing with fire, because with every passing moment, the flames were dancing higher. "I dare you to take it from me."

"You dare me, do you?" His grin inched higher.

Oh, she loved this, loved the playfulness and lightheartedness that she had with Brock. As much as she'd appreciated her friendship with Reed over the years, they'd always been so serious with each other.

She tried to pretend to be grave with Brock, frowning at him, but in the next instant, she wrapped her legs around him, locking them at her knees. Then she shoved the phone down onto the counter so that it was outside either of their grasps.

He attempted to spring after it, but the grip of her legs was too tight, halting him in place.

She wrapped her arms around him next, grasping her hands into a locked position at his back, one that would be difficult to break free from as well.

His eyes widened as he glanced down to find himself pinned by her legs and arms.

It was her turn to smile. "You're not going anywhere, buster."

"Buster?" His voice rose, as though he was offended at her name, although his grin said otherwise.

"Yes, buster. You're all mine." She tightened her hold.

"All yours?" His smile turned suddenly lopsided, and his lashes fell halfway. "Well, darlin'. If you say so." He stopped straining against her and instead relaxed so that his body sagged into her. His arms slipped around her, his hands flattening against her back.

She didn't feel in charge of the situation anymore. Even though she had him wrapped up, he'd somehow turned things around so that he was in control of her, almost as if he'd planned it.

"Now that you have me"—his voice dropped several decibels—"what will you do with me?"

Her stomach tumbled over itself, flipping and turning like a gymnast on the uneven bars. Oh, oh, oh. He was good.

He didn't wait for her answer. Instead he leaned his head in closer until his forehead came to rest against hers. His nose almost brushed hers, and his lips were within kissing distance. Not that she planned on kissing him. No sir. They were just teasing each other. That's all.

Even so, it was an intoxicating kind of teasing that made her almost giddy. She wouldn't be being honest with herself if she didn't admit that she loved the feel of his hands against her back, the way his fingers spread out as though he were claiming her. And she loved the pressure of his chest against hers, the solid length and hard muscles that met all her womanly softness.

She waited for him to tease her again. But he'd closed his eyes, seeming to relish holding her as much as she liked holding him.

Their fake relationship would be so much easier if they weren't attracted to each other. But it was obvious that the more they were together, the more the attraction was growing. Especially in this moment.

As he skimmed one of his hands up her back and toward her neck, he left a trail of flames in his wake. When he reached her neck, his fingers slid gently into her loose hair. His touch was tentative, almost reverent.

It was her turn to close her eyes as pleasure cascaded through her. How was it possible that just his fingers in her hair could affect her this much? How could his merest touch leave such an imprint? Because that's how it had been all along with him—even the smallest measures made her feel things she'd never experienced before.

She wanted to excuse away the feelings, pretend they

weren't real, blame them on the forced proximity of their situation. But deep inside, she knew the feelings were more than that. Something was there between them, something alive, something that could consume her if she weren't careful.

His breath bathed her lips, tempting her to initiate something with him, to mesh her mouth with his as she had the past couple of kisses. But there was no reason to do so. No one to perform for. No spectators. No audience.

This time, the only excuse was pure desire.

"Knock, knock." A woman's voice came from the back entryway.

Brock startled.

Venus didn't loosen her grip of either her arms or legs.

"Oh, I'm sorry," came the woman's voice with a hint of a laugh. "I didn't mean to interrupt."

Venus didn't bother to look at the newcomer. She wanted to keep going with Brock, to see where they were headed, to wait for him to kiss her.

"I'm Tia from *Rolling Stone*." The woman laughed again. "Do you want me to wait outside?"

"Yes." Venus didn't care if she sounded rude. She'd learned over the years that the only way to keep her sanity was by setting firm boundaries, and she didn't care if this reporter or photographer or whoever had to wait a few minutes longer.

Brock's eyes remained on Venus, but an easy grin slid into place. "No, course not. Come on in." He cocked a brow at Venus. No doubt he was asking if she really wanted the reporter to go away so they could finish whatever this was they'd started.

She really did. But Brock hadn't initiated any of this contact. And he also hadn't kissed her, even though he'd had every opportunity to do so. Was he holding back? Was that why he hadn't texted her all last week?

Before she threw herself on him again, and thoroughly humiliated herself in the process, maybe it was best if she found out what he was thinking about everything. Not that it mattered. Their fake relationship couldn't ever become real, could it?

"I see the reports weren't exaggerating," the woman was saying as she made her way farther into the kitchen. "There is something going on between the two of you."

Something going on was right. Venus unlocked her legs and arms from around Brock and sat up on the counter at the same time that he took a step back.

Tia seemed to pounce upon them the moment they separated. At the very least, the short woman was right there in the middle, her eyes abnormally round behind extra-large and extra-nerdy glasses as if she could see every detail and never missed anything. Venus hoped she was wrong and that the woman wasn't as keen as that.

Tia turned her attention on Brock, her eyes full of stars. Thin and pretty, with her straight black hair cropped at her shoulders, the reporter wore an oversized T-shirt with an enormous daisy filling it, ripped-up jeans, and bright yellow Converse platform sneakers.

"Ethan and I are so excited to be with you guys." Tia waved at a man lingering in the back hallway—the photographer, with a large camera hanging from his neck. "I'm hoping I can uncover all of your secrets today."

All of their secrets? That didn't sound good. Maybe meeting with the *Rolling Stone* was a bad idea after all. The interview was supposed to be another boost to both of their careers. But if Tia was smart enough, would she see through their relationship to the charade it really was?

Venus swallowed the sudden protest that rose inside her. It was too late to cancel now. The best thing to do was to keep moving forward. She cared about Brock. She liked being with him. And they did have a relationship of sorts. She wouldn't have to pretend to enjoy the day with him.

At least that much was true.

16

Brock raced along the wooded path with Venus riding him piggyback style, her laughter ringing out in the quiet of the forest.

His heart thrummed with a thousand emotions. He'd never felt this way about any other woman. The fear of choosing the wrong woman still nagged at him, but after spending another day with Venus, the worries were growing quieter and the love for her louder.

Did that mean she was the special woman he'd given up hope of finding?

"Faster, Brock!" she called through her laughter.

The late-afternoon sunshine filtered through the branches overhead, casting slanted light over them. The coolness of the woods and the slight breeze kept them from getting too hot on the sunny September day.

He halted abruptly, loving the feel of her body wrapped around him. It brought back the heat that had lain dormant since earlier in the day when they'd been in the kitchen and she'd pinned him in a hold with her legs and arms to keep him from reaching his phone.

Course, he'd let her do it. He could've gotten his phone if he'd wanted to. But Dad had always let Mom win anytime they played together. Sure, Dad had made her struggle, but in the end, he gave in and let her have her way in whatever she wanted. Brock had always loved that about Dad, the teasing that led to surrender and sweetness and never to antagonism.

"Why did you stop?" Venus bent in, her mouth near his ear.

At the breathiness of her voice, all he wanted to do was stand there, hold her, and let her nuzzle his ear.

"Am I wearing you out?" she asked.

Did he dare tell her the truth, that she was like the sun to him? Her rays were sometimes gentle and soft, sifting through the leaves. Sometimes the heat was intense and direct and burned him up. Either way, his whole world was beginning to revolve around her, and he wasn't sure he could break the gravitational pull now that he was in her orbit.

He wanted to stop and type up his thoughts—more new lyrics—but he refrained since today wasn't about writing music.

"Turn to the side just a little, Brock!" Tia called from down the trail where she and Ethan were stationed.

Ethan's camera had been a permanent fixture on his face. Brock had expected the *Rolling Stone* photographer to snap a fair share of pictures, but the guy had probably taken several thousand.

Course, Venus had been a good sport about it. She was used to posing and had done a fabulous job of giving *Rolling Stone* some excellent pictures.

Throughout it all, Brock had been determined to make the day as fun as possible for Venus. From the ropes course to the horseback ride to the archery range to the hot spring—he'd wanted her to forget about everything and just enjoy herself.

For the most part, they'd done their best to ignore Tia and Ethan—which was what Tia had wanted anyway so the photos could capture them as naturally as possible. But sometimes—like now—there was no avoiding the fact that their every move was being scrutinized.

"Angle a little more," Tia called.

Brock turned so that Ethan could see more of Venus.

"That's perfect." Tia leaned in and spoke with Ethan, nodded her head, spoke to the photographer again, then nodded some more.

"I say we finish these last pictures and call it a day," Venus suggested. "We've given them plenty to work with."

"You got that right, darlin'." Brock began to lower her.

"Hold on!" Tia called.

"We're done." Brock made sure Venus was securely on the ground before releasing his hold on her. After they'd sat in the hot spring and sipped iced coffee, Venus had changed into a light-green sundress with spaghetti straps that showed off her elegant shoulders. She'd been beautiful all day, and it hadn't mattered what she'd worn, but at the moment, with the splashes of sunlight upon her, she looked especially pretty, her long hair tied up, her cheeks flushed, and her blue eyes bright.

Tia and Ethan started up the path toward them.

Venus straightened the collar of the blue polo shirt that Brock had paired with khaki shorts. As she did so, she smiled up at him. "I messed you up."

"I don't mind, darlin'. As long as you're around to fix me, that's all that matters."

She pushed him lightly. "I'd say you're flattering me, but I know you mean it."

"Course I do."

"Sometimes"—she lowered her voice—"in all the pretending, it's hard to know what's real anymore and what's just part of the show."

He tossed a glance toward Tia, who was almost upon them. "It's not a show for me."

Venus studied his face, her expression growing more solemn.

In the next instant, Tia was upon them. "We were

hoping we could get a set of pictures of you with your guitar. Maybe sitting on the deck at your family's house. Or even sitting on one of those old wooden fences that are still up in certain places."

Brock shook his head. "Think we're tuckered out and ready to be done."

"Tuckered out?" Venus poked him in the ribs.

"Tuckered." He poked her back. "What, don't you like my word choice?"

"You sound like a country bumpkin."

"Country bumpkin?" He tickled her again. "How about a cowboy?"

"Is redneck better?"

"Nope."

She tried to wiggle out from underneath his fingers, but he was quicker and held on to her and kept tickling.

Within seconds, she was laughing and falling into his arms, and he was there for it, ready to catch and hold her. He realized he was probably smiling every bit like a country bumpkin, but he didn't care.

"You know what shot we haven't got of the two of you today?" Tia was standing back with Ethan as he snapped the camera at them during their entire exchange. "We haven't got any pictures of the two of you kissing."

Against him, Venus stiffened. That was his answer to Tia's underhanded suggestion to kiss. They weren't doing it. Not if it made Venus uncomfortable. "Sorry, guys.

That's where I'm drawing the line. Some things need to stay private, and that's one of them."

"There haven't been any recent pictures of the two of you kissing, have there?" Tia asked to no one specifically.

"No, and we don't need any," Brock responded quickly. "We've got plenty of other great pictures today."

Tia shrugged. They'd given her the basics about their relationship throughout the day whenever she stopped to ask them questions about how they'd met, first impressions, how long they'd known each other, when they'd started getting serious, and what they liked about each other. Most of the questions had been easy to answer with the truth. After all, they'd been friends for a long time through Reed and had always enjoyed hanging out together.

Tia had also taken some time to interview a few others in the family when they'd been at the house. Brock figured her prying wasn't anything to get worked up about since his family didn't know a whole lot about his dating history other than what was already out there on the internet.

Brock started to step away from Venus, to put some distance between them before he gave in and kissed her the way he'd been wanting to for days. Instead of letting him retreat, she slipped her arm through his. "I don't mind if they want to get a picture of us kissing."

The moment she spoke the words, she ducked her

head and bit her lip, almost as if she was embarrassed to admit she wouldn't mind kissing him.

Well, shoot. If taking a picture would grant him access, maybe he oughta go for it.

He slowly shifted around so that he was facing her directly. He settled both hands on her waist. Then he waited patiently—or at least tried to—for her to look up at him.

As she lifted her face and met his gaze, her expression softened, and her eyes were innocent and sweet and filled with hope, like a girl who was about to experience her first kiss.

Maybe he hadn't been her first kiss, but he could be her last—the last and only man who ever kissed her again.

He brought up a hand to her cheek and skimmed the elegant slant.

She leaned her head into his touch, her long lashes fanning out and making her eyes more luminous.

His heart tapped out a new rhythm, the melody for a new song. Not only was she his inspiration for the words he'd been writing, but she was also the inspiration for the music. Her presence went deep into his blood so that the very essence of her was pumping through him. His every breath, every heartbeat, every movement, was about her, stirring in him more love.

Even in this moment, she was everything. He wasn't sure when or where or how this consuming feeling had developed. But all day it had been building so that he was almost crazy with his need for her.

Was this what all the other McQuaid men had felt for the women they'd fallen in love with? Was this the passionate legacy of love that had been handed down to him?

Although they were kissing for an audience and for the article in *Rolling Stone*, he suddenly wanted Venus to know he wasn't pretending anymore, maybe never had been. He needed her to know that what was happening between them was real—the realest he'd ever been in his life. In fact, in some ways it felt like he'd been dreaming all these years and had woken up when she'd come along.

He'd just birthed another song with that thought, but with her beautiful eyes watching him expectantly, he wanted to be the one to initiate the kiss this time and to let her know through the kiss what he was feeling—or at least a portion of it, because he suspected it would take a lifetime and beyond to express everything he was feeling for her.

He brushed his fingers along her jaw, then along her chin. Every single part of her face was exquisite, and he could go on tracing each line and curve all day. But Tia and Ethan were waiting to get a kissing photo, and that's what he would give them—the world's best kiss.

He inched forward until his lips hovered near Venus's. She hadn't broken from his gaze yet, and something shifted in her eyes, turning the summer blue to an autumn blue, like the sky overhead. The darker blue held notes of expectation…and maybe even desire.

Did she want to kiss him as much as he did her? Was that why she'd so easily acquiesced to Tia's request?

Her hands slid up his arms, stopping on his biceps. Her fingers circled his muscles, tightened, and then she tugged him forward.

He closed the gap between their bodies, letting his press to hers, feeling every part of her in a completely new and sensitive way, as if his nerves were heightened and every inch of him raw.

Her lashes fell, and her features tightened, this time with obvious desire.

The sight of it drew upon something deep inside him, so that a soft moan welled up. Part of it filled the air between them, but the rest was stifled as he meshed his mouth to hers, releasing all the emotion he'd been feeling, uncaging everything he'd kept locked away for the past few weeks.

She didn't hesitate to respond. In fact, there was a hunger in her movements, as if she'd been waiting for his kiss, needed it, and now couldn't get enough. He didn't want to assume she was feeling the same that he was. She couldn't be. No one could experience the same depth of emotion that was running through him. But she was experiencing something. Her kiss was too passionate and eager to be pretend.

The rhythm of their mouths together was like singing in perfect harmony. She was singing the melody, and he was on the third below her, blending together in a way that was rich and beautiful. It was the best music ever created, and he didn't want the sound of it to end.

"Good!" Tia called.

The voice was off-key, jarring him back to reality.

Venus broke the kiss, then buried her face against his shoulder.

Brock wrapped his arms around her, wishing he could protect her from this public display, wanting their kisses to be private. They may have started their relationship to put on a show for everyone else, but he was done with that.

"Maybe one more." Tia's voice rang out. "This one a little slower."

Brock tossed Tia a grin. "As much as I want to kiss Venus again, I won't do any more for the cameras."

Venus didn't move but seemed to relax against him.

He bent in and pressed a kiss to her head. From the corner of his eye, he could see Ethan snapping more pictures of them. Brock inwardly sighed, then he pulled back from Venus.

"No more pictures today with Venus." Brock cocked his head in the direction of the house. "But how about I meet you back at the house in a few minutes, and I'll give you a few more shots of me with my guitar."

"Sure." Tia tugged on Ethan's camera, drawing it down from his face. "That sounds like a workable plan."

Venus stepped out of his embrace, but he kept his arm around her, and thankfully she didn't seem to mind. They stood together on the trail and watched as Tia and Ethan began to hike away. When the two turned the corner onto the long winding driveway that led to the house, Brock let himself take a deep breath.

She expelled a breath too. "Do you think they suspect we're pretending?"

He tried not to flinch, but her words punched him hard in the gut.

"In my opinion, we did a superior job with our acting all day." She smiled up at him. "Maybe when I'm done modeling, I'll go into acting. What do you think?"

A part of him knew he needed to play along with her, to grin and tease her back. But the other part of him—the part that wanted to finally be honest—pushed to the surface. "Venus, you should know…"

As if sensing the seriousness in what he was about to say, her smile faded.

He had to tell her the truth. "Today, that kiss, this time together—it hasn't been acting for me."

Her eyes flashed with something. Was it fear?

He hesitated. What if he said too much too soon and scared her away? He didn't want that to happen. On the other hand, how could he keep pretending that what he felt for her wasn't real?

He grasped her hand in his. He had to tell her. If he didn't now, he would later. So why not now? "The truth is…"

She remained silent, didn't try to interrupt him or stop him. That was a good sign, wasn't it?

"The truth is…" he started again. "I haven't been pretending for a while because I really like you." *Like?* What was he saying? His feelings for her were infinitely more than *like*.

She was searching his face as though trying to make sense of what he was saying.

"Venus." His voice dropped to a ragged whisper. "I've fallen in love with you—"

"No, Brock." She held out a hand to stop him as she took several steps away. "That wasn't part of our deal."

"I know. But it happened, and I can't keep hiding my feelings from you."

Her face had grown pale and her body stiff. "We've just been having a good time. That's all."

A vise of panic closed around his stomach. This wasn't going well, and he needed to salvage the situation. "Yes, I've had a good time with you, but I'd like more—"

She shook her head. "Remember, this is about Reed?"

"Do you still love him?" The question came out more forcefully than he'd intended. But he had to know where she stood with Reed.

17

Did she still love Reed?

Of course she did, didn't she? But he was happy with Lexi and was getting married to her.

"You love him." Brock's statement was laced with hurt, and his dark-brown eyes took on a shadow.

"You knew about my feelings for him from the start." It was the only thing she could think to say.

"But I thought after we spent time together and after getting to know me, you might like me now."

"I do like you."

"But you don't like me enough to give us a chance, to see what we could have?"

Wasn't that what her mom did? Her mom always said she needed to give the new man *a chance* to find out where things could lead. And where had the relationships led? To hurt, disappointment, and breakup. Because her mom's heart still belonged to someone else. She'd never stopped loving Marco.

Venus pressed a hand to her own heart, which in some ways still belonged to Reed. If she pursued a relationship with Brock, she'd probably end up just like her mom, playing the comparison game and unable to commit.

Reed had accused her of already being like her mom, of being unable to commit. But he was wrong. There was a big difference in that her mom jumped into every relationship that came her way, while Venus was doing her best to avoid shallow and passing relationships.

The question was—was Brock shallow and passing?

He didn't feel that way. But he also wasn't Reed, the only man in her life who hadn't left her, who'd been there for her through every hardship, who'd listened and cared and supported her.

As if her thoughts were written on her face, Brock's shoulders slumped. She wanted to hug him and tell him everything would be okay. But now that he'd confessed his love, nothing could ever be the same between them.

They wouldn't be able to pretend any longer and simply have fun, because in the back of her mind, she would know that Brock loved her and wanted more from her than just having a good time. And she couldn't give him more than just a good time right now. Maybe not ever.

"I'm sorry, Brock." Her whisper fell like a boulder

dropping into a pond, rippling out so that a cold wave crashed over her. She hugged her arms to her chest. Already she felt the distance widening between them—a distance they wouldn't be able to bridge.

"I'm sorry too," he whispered, shoving his hands deep in his pockets.

She hated that she was hurting him, but she hadn't expected him to fall in love with her, should have warned him not to, that she wasn't ready, that she couldn't reciprocate, that they could only be friends.

But it was too late for that. All she could do now was try not to cause him any more pain, and the best way to do that was to keep her distance from him.

Without waiting for him to say more, she turned on her heel and started back to the house. As she entered, she hoped she could avoid everyone. But she had no such luck. An eager Wyatt was home from school and talked to her nonstop. Anson had freshly baked cookies waiting. Leah was bright-eyed and working on a wedding task for Kinsey. And T.W. was awake and full of questions about the day.

She talked to everyone like she normally did, then while they were all distracted by Brock's photo shoot with his guitar on the deck, she quickly packed her suitcase and carry-on bag, slipped outside, and drove away, hoping no one would see her leaving.

She half expected Brock to come chasing after her,

maybe on one of the horses like in the movies when the hero rushed after the heroine and declared his love for her. But as she wound through Healing Springs Ranch, no one appeared in her rearview mirror.

She was well on her way up the passes en route to Colorado Springs before the first calls started coming in from Brock, then T.W., and even Leah. Venus didn't answer any of them, didn't want them to try to convince her to return.

It was best if she and Brock each went their separate ways. He could spend the rest of the week in Aruba, and she'd head back to New York and let Kristin know she could start work again a few days early.

Yes, she would be breaching the contract she'd signed with Brock's people regarding the terms of the fake relationship. But in the long run, no one would really care if she and Brock spent time together. They'd already proven to the world they were a couple and had made enough appearances. Besides, the *Rolling Stone* article would come out soon and promote them as a couple too.

When she was seated in first class on her flight to New York City, she responded to just one person—Reed. They'd been texting more since their lunch last week, and she'd told him all about the upcoming vacation with Brock and about the *Rolling Stone* interview.

Reed: *How was the photo shoot?*

Venus: *Fun. Lots of great pics.*

Reed: 👍

Venus: *I left the vacay early.*

Reed: *Why? Everything ok?*

She blinked back a sudden swell of tears. Everything had been fun and going well until Brock had gotten serious. Why had he told her he loved her? From the gravity in his expression, she guessed it hadn't been easy to bring up his feelings. And she'd been callous back. But what else should she have done?

Reed: *???*

Venus: *I'm ok.*

Reed: *You sure?*

No, she wasn't okay. More tears stung the backs of her eyes. She'd really liked Brock, had loved his family, had been enjoying their time together, and had actually been looking forward to a few days in Aruba with him. She'd anticipated more fun and adventures along with good conversations and good food on beautiful beaches with him by her side.

But she couldn't spend the vacation with him now. Not after what he'd said. Maybe not even after the kiss. Because if she was completely honest, the kiss had shifted something between them too. It had been filled with too much longing and need and emotions to be casual. In hindsight, none of the kisses with Brock had been casual, but this one had been particularly poignant and had contained a deeper meaning, probably his love.

> **Reed:** *Talk to me.*
>
> **Venus:** *Brock told me he loved me.*
>
> **Reed:** *Wow. Didn't think he was capable.*
>
> **Venus:** *I don't know what to do.*
>
> **Reed:** *Do you love him back?*
>
> **Venus:** *Not yet.*

But did she love Brock back? Even as the airplane prepared to pull away from the gate, she pressed her hand to her chest to ease the ache that was growing inside. She could admit she cared for him, that there were a lot of qualities about him she really liked.

And he treated her so well, was always respectful and considerate and sweet.

She'd never been around a guy who was so attentive the way Brock was, like everything she said, did, and thought was important. The only word she could use to describe his attitude was *cherish*. Yes, he cherished her.

Had any man ever cherished her? Certainly not Marco, who'd never been in her and Mom's lives. Certainly not all the other men Mom had been with.

Certainly not any of the men Venus had dated who'd only cared about her body.

Had Reed cherished her?

Reed: It's ok not to love him back.

Venus: But he's a great guy.

Reed: Knowing Brock he'll move on.

She wasn't ready for Brock to move on. In fact, the very thought of him going out with any other woman made her dizzy, and she closed her eyes again. She might not love him—at least, not yet—but she also wasn't ready to let go of him.

That wasn't fair to him. But maybe after her rejection and then leaving without a goodbye, he'd decide he'd dodged a bullet and was better off without her.

Was it finally time to come clean with Reed about the true nature of her relationship with Brock? She wanted to, didn't want to hide it and then have him find out later and be hurt.

She hesitated only a moment longer, then she started typing.

Venus: We weren't really dating.

Reed: Huh?

Venus: Our managers made the arrangements.

Reed: So it wasn't a real relationship?

Venus: Right.

Reed: *Then why did he tell you he loved you?*

Venus: *Because he said it became real for him.*

Reed: *Real for ten seconds since he doesn't know what real love is.*

Was Reed right? Brock had a reputation of moving on from women, never being able to commit. That was why she'd agreed to fake date him in the first place, because of Ainsley Rose's accusations that he didn't want to get serious.

Maybe Brock thought he loved her now. But in a few days or a few weeks, he'd just break up with her and find someone new. Because Reed was right. That was Brock's pattern.

The announcement to turn off devices came over the airplane's speakers.

Venus: *Gotta go.*

Reed: *Ok. Love you.*

Venus: *Love you too.*

Why was it so easy to tell Reed she loved him? They'd been exchanging the words for years, and it had worked out fine for them.

Except that deep inside, she knew Brock's declaration was different. It went beyond friendship. It even went beyond a typical dating relationship. She'd felt something in the way he'd kissed her, the way he'd held her, even the way he'd looked at her. She hadn't wanted to acknowledge it at the time, had tried to ignore it, but his feelings for her had been genuine and alive and powerful.

Maybe that's why she'd been so scared. Because she didn't know what to do in response…except to run away. She'd hoped that confessing everything to Reed would help bring a sense of balance back to her life and ground her.

Why, then, did she feel as though she'd been knocked from her feet and was floating aimlessly?

18

"Have you heard from her yet?"

Dad's question jarred Brock awake. He sat up straight, nearly dropping his guitar.

Where was he, and what was going on in his life?

As he opened his eyes, the pain in his chest came rushing back with a force that made him breathless. Pain because Venus had left him last night. While he'd been busy, she'd driven away without saying goodbye or why she was leaving—although he hadn't needed an explanation. He already knew that she hadn't liked that he'd told her he loved her, and she'd run away from him because of it.

Why had he done it?

He leaned forward in the recliner beside his dad's hospital bed, set aside his guitar, and braced his head in his hands. His head ached almost as much as his heart.

"Check your phone," Dad insisted, reclining in bed

with a steaming cup of coffee already in hand, a newspaper in the other, and his reading glasses perched on his nose.

Brock glanced at his screen. Only another text from Ella Mae, this one confirming the flight details for Aruba. "Nothing."

"Shoot." Dad's voice hinted at disappointment. "I thought for sure she'd miss you by now and reach out."

Brock just groaned. He needed to come clean and admit that the whole relationship had been a sham from the start and that's why Venus didn't miss him. But he still couldn't make himself say the truth.

All night, like his dad, he'd been waiting for her text and holding out hope that she'd realize what she'd left behind, that she'd admit she had feelings for him after all.

But she hadn't said one word. All Ella Mae and Harper had learned after finally reaching Venus's agent last night was that she'd decided to return to New York City early and get back to work, especially with how busy her schedule had become. Kristin had indicated that because of such a full workload, all dates and time together would be suspended for the time being.

Brock had wanted to protest. He'd even halfway considered Harper's suggestion to force Venus to honor their contract and finish out the vacation in Aruba and then continue the once-a-week dates.

But Brock didn't want to spend time with Venus that

way. He wanted her willingly or not at all. As it turned out, she was breaking all ties with him. That had become clear.

"Try calling her again." Dad took a slurp of his coffee. He was still attired in his pajamas and was probably waiting for Kinsey to come in and take his vitals.

"Dad." Brock expelled a tight breath through his constricted lungs. "I've tried calling her at least twenty times and have left as many messages and texts."

"You can't give up."

"I'm not."

"Then keep calling and keep texting."

"I'll try again later."

"Try now."

"Dad. Please." Brock pushed up from the chair, bumping his guitar. He'd tried to focus on the newest song last night, had thought he'd at least write some chords. But his brain hadn't been able to come up with more than a few notes, and even those had sounded discordant.

The simple truth was that he didn't want to make music if she wasn't in his life. He didn't want to breathe or eat or do anything.

He crossed to the window that overlooked the eastern range. With the morning sunlight slanting over the mountain peaks, he could only picture Venus as they'd watched the sunrise together and how the rays had finally fallen upon her, turning her into a golden goddess. That whole night together and that morning had been perfect.

Why couldn't she see that? Why couldn't she see how perfect every day together had been, including yesterday? Even with the *Rolling Stone* people following them around, he'd loved every minute with her. He'd thought she'd enjoyed the day too.

Everything had been going great until he'd said the L-word. On some level, he'd known she wouldn't reciprocate yet, had known his feelings had happened fast and furiously and that she would need more time.

What he hadn't expected was her admission that she was still in love with Reed and, as a result, wasn't interested in pursuing anything else.

Brock leaned his forehead against the windowpane, the cool glass soothing his overheated face but doing nothing to take away the throbbing in his head and chest and whole body.

He'd lost her.

No, he'd never really had her to begin with. Not when their whole relationship had been based on a lie. Why had he ever thought anything good could come out of lying?

"If you really love her, then you need to do more." Dad's voice was as strong and healthy and pushy as always. Even if he was still battling fatigue and poor appetite from his chemotherapy and wasn't the same robust man that he'd been a year or two ago, he was proving himself to be stalwart in his matchmaking. "You can't just sit back and wait for her to initiate. No, we McQuaid men fight hard to keep the women we love."

Growing up, Brock had heard the story more times than he could count of how Dad had won Mom. As Miss Colorado, Mom had been traveling around the state to promote her platform to preserve Colorado wildlife. She'd protested Dad's ranch and his drilling of oil there because some of the practices were interfering with the natural habitat for many of the creatures in the area. Mom had considered Dad her enemy. But as Dad liked to say, he'd worked hard to win her over, even going as far as changing all his drilling methods in spite of the expense in doing so.

"Fight for her," Dad said again. "That's what you need to do now."

Brock had already explained to his dad and mom and siblings what had happened during their last moments of the photo shoot, how he'd told Venus he loved her and she'd run off. He hadn't been able to hold back, had been too upset at the time. But now, a part of him wished he'd kept the breakup with Venus to himself and made up an excuse to his family for why she'd left so suddenly— although he suspected they probably would have seen through any excuses he made.

"If I do more, Dad, I might end up pushing her away

even further."

"She'll see your efforts to win her and eventually realize you love her enough and won't let her get away."

"She might just need some time."

"Maybe. But she might also need to know how serious you are about your relationship."

"I think she knows. I made it pretty clear."

Dad blew out an exasperated breath. "Sounds to me like you're giving up."

"How can I give up something that was never mine to begin with?"

"What's that supposed to mean?"

Brock clamped his mouth closed and shook his head. The conversation with his dad was going the way lots of conversations had gone. He wasn't doing what his dad wanted, couldn't live up to the expectations. It had been this way all along, his being unable to live up to the standards his dad set for him.

He'd disappointed Dad when he'd graduated from college and refused to come back to the ranch and work like Ty had done. He'd disappointed Dad when he'd taken the record deal in Nashville. He'd disappointed Dad when he'd gained his reputation as a womanizer. He'd disappointed Dad when he'd bought his ranch in Tennessee instead of Colorado. He'd disappointed Dad when he'd turned twenty-nine and still hadn't settled down.

He actually couldn't think of one thing Dad had approved of. All Brock had ever done was make Dad shake his head and roll his eyes and mutter under his breath. And if he refused Dad's advice now about Venus, he'd only earn more disapproval.

He turned around and faced Dad. "Listen, Dad. I know over the years I haven't done things the way you've wanted and have disappointed you."

"That's not true—"

"It is true. And the fact is, I'm gonna have to disappoint you again."

"C'mon, Brock—"

"I've done what I can, and I'm letting Venus go." He couldn't keep pushing Venus. He'd done all he could to win her over. Now it was time to step away.

Dad fell silent.

Even in the silence, Brock could feel the heavy weight of dissatisfaction rolling off his dad.

"I'm sorry that my way isn't what the McQuaid men would do. And I'm sorry I'm not living up to the legacy. But I guess I'm the one failure of the bunch."

"We all have times where we fail, but that doesn't make us a failure."

No matter how his dad phrased things, Brock knew he'd failed. He made his way back to the bedside chair, picked up his guitar, then paused next to his dad. "I need to head out. You keep getting better, okay?"

"Don't leave like this, Brock." Dad put out a hand to stop him.

Brock sidestepped his dad and started toward the door. "I'll be fine."

But even as he told himself he'd be fine, something deep inside told him that this time he wouldn't be fine. Not after losing Venus. After losing her, he'd never be fine again.

19

She didn't want to be in Los Cabos for Reed's bachelor party.

Venus stood on the private patio of her resort suite and tried to enjoy the view of the ocean with its cobalt water, white sands, tropical plants, and palm trees. But she was too tense.

Not that she didn't like visits to the tropical paradise. She'd been there before on vacations with her mom. She'd come with girlfriends after graduating from high school. She'd even been there a couple of times to model swimwear.

But this time was different.

A gentle evening breeze filled with the scent of salt and sea caressed her skin. She shivered and drew her light sweater closed over her sundress.

Reed was really going through with his marriage to Lexi. Since the engagement in early August, he hadn't changed his mind. He hadn't wavered. And he hadn't hinted that maybe he was having second thoughts, even though he'd admitted to being jealous a few weeks ago in New York.

"It's okay," she whispered. If Reed was still in love with Lexi and felt certain he was doing the right thing, then Venus had to stop hoping he'd want her instead. She'd known that from the start of his engagement. She didn't want to break him and Lexi up, didn't want to cause him heartache, didn't want to interfere. "He loves Lexi. She'll make him happy. And that's all that matters."

Was it finally time to accept that she and Reed would never be more than friends? That, in fact, she was okay with just friendship?

Because she was…

Venus took in the stunning view for a last long second, then she turned away from it, back to her suite with the king-sized bed in the spacious bedroom with the high ceiling fan, walk-in closet, and sitting area.

She paused and waited for the jealousy, the hurt, or even the frustration over Reed and Lexi to swell inside her. But there was nothing. Except the tension. If she was honest with herself, the tension had nothing to do with Reed or Lexi. It had everything to do with the fact that Brock McQuaid was coming to the bachelor party too.

Over two weeks had passed since she'd driven away from Healing Springs Ranch and Brock. And she hadn't talked to him once in all that time. Not that he hadn't reached out to try to talk with her. He had.

That first night, he'd left voicemail after voicemail telling her he was sorry and that he didn't want to lose her. He'd had both Ella Mae and Harper call and text her too. Eventually Brock had gotten Venus's unspoken message that she didn't want to talk. After that night, he hadn't called or texted again.

She'd heard through her agent that he'd gone to Aruba for a few days and then to his ranch in Nashville. No doubt he'd been busy writing songs for his new album.

Was she still his inspiration?

She gave a sharp shake of her head. No, it didn't matter. Of course she wouldn't be his inspiration anymore. She was being ridiculous to even think that was a possibility. Not after the way she'd cut him out of her life.

"I've fallen in love with you…and I'd like more." His words were like a playlist on repeat, and no matter what she'd done to shut out the music, the melody hummed through her head.

Brock had fallen in love with her. He loved her.

The more she'd repeated it, the more it had seemed to sink in that a handsome and successful man like Brock McQuaid loved her. He was everything any woman could ever dream of having. Of course, he wasn't perfect, but he was an honorable man in all the ways that counted. And he'd been so, so good to her.

The truth was, she'd missed him since leaving the ranch, and she felt as though a part of her was empty without him. She'd been unusually sad, even despondent, knowing she'd never be with him again in the same way.

She'd tried to ignore the ache inside, but it had been deepening with every passing day, and now that she would see him tonight, she wasn't sure what to do with herself.

A text dinged on her phone.

She crossed to the bed, where she'd tossed her phone and the rest of the contents of her travel bag when she'd arrived. She flipped the phone over and took in the name. Kristin.

She bit back a sigh. Who had she hoped would be texting her? Brock? Of course he wouldn't be.

Venus started to fling her phone back onto the bed, but another text came through from Kristin with the first few words showing.

Kristin: *Look at the article!...*

Venus's heart crashed to a halt. Kristin could only be talking about one article—the *Rolling Stone* piece that was due to release today. Venus had been waiting for it, worrying that Tia and Ethan had seen right through her and Brock's charade.

In fact, Venus wished she hadn't agreed to the interview. It had been a bad idea to make their fake relationship so public. Even if doing so would give them lots of publicity now, in the long run, what would happen once word got around that she and Brock were no longer seeing each other?

It was bound to happen. Maybe not anytime soon, because they would both be at the bachelor party and the wedding. But eventually, the two of them would need to stage an official breakup.

Maybe it would be sooner rather than later if the *Rolling Stone* article picked up on their fakeness…

She tapped the link in Kristin's text, and her browser opened up to the digital version of the article to find the big bold title: *Brock McQuaid Head Over Boot Heels.*

Tia had obviously played on one of Brock's hit songs to create the title, like most articles did.

Venus read the subtitle: *No doubt about it, the man is in love.* That was a line from another one of Brock's songs. Venus knew because she'd listened to only his music for the past two weeks. She'd told herself doing so was harmless, that she simply liked his songs, that it didn't mean anything. But it had made her think about him all the more.

She blew out an exasperated sigh—one directed at herself. Why had she cut things off with him so completely? She could have at least maintained their friendship.

Maybe this weekend she could find a way to talk to him. Should she apologize? At the very least, she could tell him she was sorry for leaving his house so abruptly without a goodbye or even a thank-you.

She hovered over the front page of the article. Brock was at the center with his guitar in hand, a mountain peak behind him. His fingers were splayed over the strings, his head bent, his scruffy jaw all that was visible of his face. But it was enough to see how ruggedly handsome he was.

She read the title again. *Brock McQuaid Head Over Boot Heels.*

It didn't have a question mark. Tia wasn't asking if Brock was head over heels. She was declaring it for the world to hear.

Did that mean Tia believed they were in love?

Venus swiped the screen to turn to the next page of the article. There, the very first picture, was the last one Ethan had taken, where she and Brock had been hugging, and he'd leaned down and kissed her head.

The photo had an almost ethereal look to it, the blue sky hazy with afternoon sunlight and clouds, the trees a blurred bright green in the background, and the two of them standing in the wilderness. Her face was buried against his shoulder, but his handsome features were in the direct line of the camera.

His lashes were half down, but his expression took her breath away. The adoration and the reverence—the emotions were so stark and so obvious that Venus could only stare.

Tia had picked a perfect title and subtitle. Brock really did seem in love—so in love that Venus's heart picked up its pace at the way he was looking at her.

It was just as he'd said. He hadn't pretended to be in a relationship just to satisfy fans. And he wasn't manufacturing emotions so he could prove he was capable of being committed to one woman. No, he looked genuine, real, and happy.

Happy. She'd been happy too. Happier than she'd ever been. Yes, even happier than she'd been with Reed.

Why? How was it possible that being with Brock brought her more happiness? Maybe because Brock was fun-loving and easygoing. He was creative and impulsive, and they had made some great memories together.

She didn't read what Tia had written and instead scrolled to the next page of the article, which was a collage of more pictures from that day together. In each one, Brock was looking at her as if she was the most important person in his world, as if no one and nothing else mattered.

Most weren't poses but were of the two of them interacting naturally—her laughing at something he'd said, him winking at her, the two of them standing shoulder to shoulder and gazing at the scenery. The one of them in the hot spring with her sitting on his lap made them look a little too cozy. She couldn't remember that picture being taken, and she was embarrassed by the seductive look on her face, as if she was thinking thoughts about Brock she shouldn't have been.

It was the one picture she wouldn't have approved of if she'd been given a choice, but she hadn't been. Now it was out there for the world to see that she was attracted to Brock McQuaid.

She released the breath she hadn't known she'd been holding. What did it matter if the world believed she was attracted to Brock? Wasn't that the point of the article?

Besides, she only had one picture showing her blatant desire for Brock, but he had six or eight revealing his feelings for her. What would he think when he saw the article? Would he be frustrated that he'd allowed himself to fall for her so quickly only to have it all thrown back in his face?

He had told her that his love hadn't been pretend, that he hadn't been acting. This article was the proof, wasn't it?

Another text from Kristin pinged on her phone.

Kristin: *The Rolling Stone pictures of the two of you are trending.*

Venus's legs turned weak, and she sank to the edge of the bed. She didn't care that the article and the pictures were trending and would push her into an even greater spotlight. That didn't matter. What mattered was figuring out what this all meant. Had she been too hasty in pushing Brock away? Should she have given them more of a chance?

She buried her face in her hands.

"No." She shoved up from the bed and straightened her shoulders. "I'm being so selfish."

She'd already cut things off with Brock, and she couldn't start up their relationship again. Not that he'd even want to—not after her complete silence since she'd run away from him, not when she still hadn't worked through her fears of becoming like her mom.

She wanted to. And she was finally beginning to admit that Reed had been correct at his engagement party when he'd accused her of being afraid of committing. She'd assumed she was waiting for Reed, had always thought he was the right person, that no one else could match up to him. But what if he'd just been an excuse to keep from committing to anyone?

She opened her phone again to the *Rolling Stone* article, to the front picture of Brock. His fingers on the guitar strings were strong and deft and calloused. The veins and sinews showed prominently, as did the smattering of dark hair on his arms where his sleeve was rolled up and one of his tattoos was visible.

She loved every detail about him and suddenly couldn't get enough. She swiped to the next page and hungrily took in each picture of him, needing him and wanting him in a way that was almost frightening. A way she'd never felt for Reed.

She'd thought by sticking with Reed and avoiding other relationships she would prevent herself from becoming like her mom. But was it possible she'd ended up doing the very same thing as her mom in elevating one man too high and comparing everyone else to him?

Venus fingered the picture of Brock in front of her. Was it time to stop letting Reed take up so much of her life? Stop holding him up as the standard she wanted?

She stood and paced to the door and then back to the bed. The truth was, she had to take this step if she really wanted to break free from the pattern her mom had modeled. She had to let go of her fears and move on…and she really did want to do that with Brock.

She could only hope she wasn't too late and hadn't pushed him entirely away. He might be mad at her, might have decided good riddance, might have made up his mind that she was too much of a hassle.

But she had to at least try to talk to him. It would be difficult with Reed and all the other guys around. But she needed to make the next move. That much was clear.

20

Maybe he shouldn't have come.

Brock stood with Reed's friends and groomsmen in the palm-thatched bar overlooking the mirrored infinity pool. The view was amazing, with the ocean spreading out beyond the pool and the darkening evening sky laced with pink and purple. The live band on the opposite side of the bar was providing cultural music, and the scent of the seafood made his stomach growl.

The resort was posh and mostly private. His room was peaceful, with an ocean view. The staff had been polite, and he'd been assigned his own butler for the stay, as was the custom for all guests.

He couldn't complain. Even so, he'd been second-guessing his decision to join in Reed's bachelor party all day, even after his jet had taken off from Nashville. He'd started half a dozen texts to Reed on the way to Los Cabos with one excuse or another for changing his plans.

But in the end, he'd deleted every single one and finally put his phone away.

The truth was, the lure to see Venus was too great to resist. And he was obviously a glutton for punishment, because being around her would be torture. But staying away when he had the chance to be near her would also be torture.

Either way, he was in a losing situation, just as he'd been since she'd left him.

He pretended to grin at something one of the others said, but he could hardly concentrate on anything, was too keyed up waiting for Venus to make her appearance. Since Reed hadn't come down yet to the oceanfront area where they were having dinner, Brock guessed Reed and Venus must be hanging out. Seeing them together would only remind him of how she'd rejected him because she still cared about Reed.

Acid rose up in his throat, and he took a sip of his Mountain Dew. He needed to go. He would never make it through the evening, much less the weekend.

He'd hardly been able to survive at his ranch over the past week, had gone crazy thinking about her and wanting to be with her. Even though he'd tried to stay busy with friends and all the things he loved about his ranch, she'd invaded every thought in almost every activity during every second. She'd even crowded his sleep and dreams.

Yep, he'd been a fool to come.

He took another drink and glanced at the pathway that led to the lobby. Maybe he should have his butler pack his bags and alert his pilot that he wanted to leave.

A hand clamped his shoulder. "So, head over boot heels, huh?" Dallas, Reed's lead guitar player, grinned at him, his leathery face crinkled. As usual, Dallas had secured his long brown-gray hair in a ponytail.

"Yep. That's me." Brock had glanced at the *Rolling Stone* article for only a second before he'd swiped it closed earlier in the afternoon. Looking at the pictures with Venus in his arms, holding her hand, sitting together in the hot spring, riding horses side by side, had been too much. Emotion had swelled swiftly and keenly, swamping him with such need for her that he'd had to close his eyes, breathe deeply, and force down the pain that had burned through him.

"You're the man." Dallas slapped Brock on the arm. "Don't know how you did it, but she's head over boot heels for you too. Although I don't know why she fell for an ugly coot like you."

Brock laughed and so did the other men around him. But at the same time, his heart sank.

How should he explain his and Venus's relationship now? And how were they supposed to interact with each other this weekend?

Brock hadn't thought that far ahead. Now, with the

Rolling Stone article out there, most people—including Reed's friends and groomsmen—would expect him and Venus to be really close and serious about each other.

He definitely shouldn't have come.

As the other men teased him about the article and claimed she'd lassoed him, he finished his drink and tried to banter back. All the while, the panic inside him kept growing. He had to get away before she made her appearance. Because if he was standing there when she showed up, everyone was sure to see that something was wrong.

Even though Reed's bachelor party was small—not more than twenty guys—the other guests and staff would be watching him and Venus too. Although the resort had a rule that prohibited guests from taking photos of the celebrities that stayed here, the gossip would find a way to the media regardless.

As soon as the conversation shifted toward one of the other men, Brock backed up and tried to make his getaway. He was stopped only a couple of times as he wound down the pathway past palm trees and exotic flowering plants. Excuses raced through his head— anything plausible that he could tell Reed for why he couldn't stay.

Not that his friend would care if he left. In fact, Reed probably hadn't wanted to invite him to the bachelor party in the first place. No doubt Reed's manager had insisted on it and had encouraged the friendship the same way Harper had.

Brock flung open the lobby door and stepped inside only to nearly barrel into the man in question.

Reed took a quick step back. "Hey, Brock." Attired in casual shorts and a button-down shirt that had palm trees on it, Reed looked relaxed and ready for a night of fun. His sandy-blond hair was damp and slicked back, and his face was clean-shaven, revealing a tan, probably from a day out in the sun riding ATVs on the beach with the other men.

If Reed was here, then Venus had to be nearby. Brock's pulse raced, and his gaze shot around the elegant lobby while his body tightened with the need to see her.

She was always easy to spot, not only because of how beautiful she was but because she carried herself with such poise and grace and confidence. As his gaze flitted around from one person to the next, he didn't see her.

Disappointment mingled with desperation. He'd thought for sure she would arrive to dinner with Reed. So where was she?

He needed to see her before he left. If he could get a glimpse of her face, look into her eyes, and maybe earn a small smile, then maybe he'd be able to leave without feeling such a huge aching hole in his chest.

"Where you headed?" Reed's brows rose, and his tone carried an edge.

"I'm sorry, Reed." Brock tried to rein in his pulse and his thoughts. "I'm happy for you and Lexi and wish I could stay to celebrate with you, but I've gotta go…"

Reed nodded. "Don't worry about it."

"I'm sure you'll have fun."

"No doubt about it."

"Good."

Reed glanced toward the elevators nervously. Almost as if he didn't want Brock to be there when the elevator doors opened. Because Venus was coming.

Brock's pulse spurted again. At that moment, the elevator dinged, and the doors began to slide open.

"Venus told me everything," Reed said quickly.

Brock didn't want to take his gaze off the elevator, but something in Reed's tone drew him. "Everything?" What did that mean?

"That you told her you loved her but that she doesn't love you back."

At her lack of love stated so plainly, Brock's gut twisted.

"She also told me that you didn't have a real relationship, that it was all arranged by your managers." Reed's expression was slightly smug.

Brock didn't know what to say. A part of him was hurt that Venus had shared their private information with Reed. But another part of him understood why she'd done so. Reed was her best friend, and she'd needed someone to confide in. After all, he'd almost told his dad and his family.

He still hadn't answered the text from his dad from last week, the one where he'd apologized for pushing Brock with Venus. The last words of the text had sifted around Brock's mind all week: *Everyone's love story is different. I'm sorry for trying to write it my way instead of letting you write it yours.*

"Listen," Reed said, dropping his voice. "It's hard not to fall for Venus, but she needs someone who can give her the love she deserves."

Brock's spine stiffened with an irrational spurt of jealousy. "And who exactly is that someone, Reed? Is it you? Because last I checked, you were getting married to Lexi."

"Or course it's not me. But it's definitely not you, either." Reed glanced in the direction of the elevator.

Brock followed his gaze and found himself looking at Venus. She'd exited the elevator, taken several steps, but now stood absolutely motionless in the flow of other guests moving around her.

She was as stunning as always in a sleek sundress that covered one shoulder and left the other bare. The slit in the skirt left a long portion of her leg showing. Her hair was twisted into an updo that revealed more of her exquisite skin.

Even from the distance across the lobby, Brock felt

the inevitable sizzle that sparked every time they were together. Maybe Reed was right, that it was hard not to fall for Venus. Maybe every guy felt chemistry with her. And maybe the best thing to do was to let her find someone else—someone she could love, because she obviously didn't love him. She'd actually told Reed that she didn't love him back, and if that wasn't humiliating, Brock didn't know what was.

Regardless of what he should or shouldn't do, he was as captivated by her as always. Her wide blue eyes held his with a power that made him forget every reason why he'd been about to leave the resort. He was suddenly breathless and needed to talk to her and touch her and be near her.

He took a step, but Reed grasped his arm and halted him.

"I thought you had to go," Reed said, straining to hold Brock back.

Yep, he needed to tuck his tail between his legs, admit defeat, and return home. He'd had his shot with Venus, and he couldn't grovel at her feet, begging her to give them a chance the way he had in his numerous voicemails.

He was tempted to call himself a failure again, especially recently, because his thoughts had been dark and his inspiration gone and even his desire to sing was absent. He hadn't been able to stop from wondering if he'd end up a failure in his career just as he'd been a failure in love.

But if this was his story that he was writing for both love and life, then why did he have to settle for failure? Maybe he wouldn't do everything the same way his dad had done, and maybe his choices would be a disappointment to his dad. But ultimately, he had to write his story his way and in his time.

Brock fisted his hands at his sides. He'd already fought hard for Venus, and for now he had to let her go, the same way he had when she'd left the ranch. The best thing was to stick with his decision to leave Los Cabos.

He tugged free from Reed's hold. "I'm heading on out."

"I'll see you at the wedding?"

"I don't think it's a good idea for me to be there, do you?"

"Probably not."

With that, Brock gave Reed a last nod, then he strode toward the elevators but kept a distance from Venus. Even then, he couldn't avoid passing by her, and he refused to ignore her. He wasn't that kind of guy. He also cared about her too much to pretend to be cold.

He slowed just a little and tried to give her a smile that felt more like a grimace. "Hey there, darlin'." The words *I missed you and I love you and I can't live without you* were on the tip of his tongue. But somehow, he managed to bite them back.

"Hi." Her response was breathless. Was it also filled with longing? Was that longing in her eyes—her stunning blue eyes that matched the clear blue ocean water?

He nearly stumbled but managed to keep himself from going down like an idiot. "Hope you have a great time this weekend."

Her brow furrowed.

He forced himself to keep walking and head toward the elevators. With each step, he felt her gaze searing into him.

"Are you leaving?" Her question finally came.

"Yep. Heading out right now." He halted at one of the elevator doors and tapped the arrow going up.

"But we all just got here, and the party hasn't even started." Did her voice have a note of desperation to it?

He couldn't keep himself from turning around and facing her.

The lines in her forehead and around her eyes made her look distressed. Was she upset he was leaving, or was something else going on? "You all right, darlin'?"

21

After how callous she'd been to him, he was asking *her* if she was all right?

Tears pricked Venus's eyes. That was just like Brock. He thought about her needs and how she was feeling above anything else.

He'd ditched his cowboy boots and faded jeans for shorts and Birkenstock sandals with his tight T-shirt. His dark hair looked like it had been recently trimmed but was still unruly. And his jaw had a five-o'clock shadow.

He looked so good. And she just wanted to stand and stare at him and take him in all night.

But he was leaving.

"Why?" She managed the one word.

He cocked a brow.

"Because of me?" She didn't care that she'd jumped to a different subject and was confusing him. She had to keep him from going, at least for a little while.

With a furrowed brow, Reed began to cross toward her. They'd been on their way to dinner, but she'd only made it to the elevators near her room when she'd realized she'd forgotten her wrap. She'd told Reed to go on down without her, that she'd be along shortly. When she'd stepped out of the elevator, the last thing she'd expected to see was Reed talking with Brock.

The conversation hadn't looked too pleasant.

"Come on." Reed halted and held out a hand toward her. "Everyone's waiting."

She ignored him and instead focused on Brock. "You came all this way. You can't leave yet."

His smile dimmed, and his brown eyes held sadness, maybe even tiredness. "I think it's for the best, especially after the article's release today. I don't want everything to be awkward."

What had he thought of the article and all the pictures? She wanted to ask him. But wouldn't that be inappropriate and insensitive of her?

He dropped his gaze from her and focused on the marble floor.

"Venus," Reed said more firmly. "Brock's trying to do the right thing. Just let him go."

The right thing?

"How do you know what the right thing is?" What she really wanted to know was how much Reed truly cared about her happiness and her feelings and how she was doing. Because one thing was for certain: he didn't treat her the same way Brock did—like she was the most precious item in the world. Which he was still doing even after she'd hurt him.

He was one very special man. Now that he was here in front of her, she didn't want to be away from him. She wanted to talk to him and be with him and find out how he was doing and what songs he'd written and how he was enjoying his time off from being on tour.

Reed's eyes flashed with warning. "Don't do this now."

"Do what?"

He glanced around to make sure most of the other guests were out of range. A few near the door were staring at the three of them, but otherwise they were out of earshot of everyone. Reed lowered his voice. "Don't drag out the breakup with Brock. Just let him go."

Brock hadn't moved, except that his jaw twitched.

Was she dragging out the breakup with Brock? Even if she was, she at least had to apologize to him before he left. "I'd like the chance to talk to Brock."

"Fine. Go ahead." Reed didn't move, as if he planned to stay and listen to the conversation.

Had Reed always been this bossy? As a friend, maybe she'd appreciated his decisiveness and quick thinking and concern. But those weren't qualities she wanted in the man she fell in love with. She wanted someone like Brock, who valued her needs, respected her decisions, and considered her an equal.

Who was she kidding? She didn't just want someone *like* Brock. She wanted *him*. Because the truth was clear, and she couldn't keep hiding behind the insecurities from her past. She'd already fallen in love with Brock. She'd just been too scared to admit it.

But if she didn't admit it, she would lose him.

She took a step away from Reed toward Brock. "I need to speak with Brock. Alone."

"And let him try to convince you again?" Reed scoffed. "No, thank you."

She closed the distance so that she was standing beside Brock.

He held himself rigidly, his broad shoulders stiff, his jaw tight, and his eyes hard upon Reed.

She wanted to place a hand on Brock's arm, but she held herself back. She had no right to…yet…and maybe not ever. But she had to see if he could forgive her and give her a second chance. "You're wrong, Reed. I'm the one who needs to convince Brock."

At her statement, Brock's gaze swung to her and the intensity of his eyes raked over her.

Her entire body longed for him again—longed to be in his arms, against his chest, and wrapped up tight. "Will you talk with me?"

"Course I will, darlin'." His words held a warmth that

she desperately needed at the moment.

"This is ridiculous," Reed said, his voice laced with irritation.

Irritation of her own flared toward her friend. "Be sensitive. If you care about me and my happiness, then wouldn't you want me to talk to him?"

Reed held her gaze for a few heartbeats before sighing. "You're right. But don't be long, and don't fall for his charm."

It was too late. She'd already fallen for Brock's charm fully and completely. She'd fallen for everything about him.

Reed narrowed a look at Brock before turning and stalking across the lobby toward the door that led to the oceanfront bar where everyone was congregated.

Once she was alone with Brock, she was tempted to fidget with her bracelet or an earring or even with her hair. But her training as a model not to squirm but to stay poised came into use. Instead, she gripped her clutch more firmly, then nodded in the direction of an opposite door that led to the beach.

"Will you walk with me?" She was afraid to meet his gaze, afraid of seeing rejection or hurt or even the sadness again. "I'd be grateful for a few minutes of your time."

He gave her one of his lopsided grins. "I can't turn down spending time with you."

"Thank you. I know you were just about to leave."

He held out his arm to her. "I'll do anything for you, darlin'. All you have to do is ask."

Did his words have a hidden meaning? Was he hinting at something deeper? She could only pray so.

She tucked her hand into his arm, circling his bicep. Oh, how she liked his bicep, with its solidness and strength—just like who he was inside, so solid and strong.

As they walked outside, the evening sky was streaked with the remnants of the setting sun, and a soft breeze took away the glaring heat from earlier in the day. The flagstone path led through palm trees and wound past a pool until at last the sandy beach spread out before them. A few other couples were strolling along the water's edge, but the busy crowds sunbathing during the day were gone, and she and Brock were mostly alone.

"I've been waiting to talk to you," she said as they ambled along the waterfront, away from the resort.

"I'm nervous." He matched his stride to hers. "Will I like what you have to say, or will it drive me crazy?"

"I hope you'll like it." With the sand filling her sandals, she slipped them off.

Before she could reach for them, Brock swiped them up. "I'll carry them."

"You don't have to."

"I want to." He tucked her hand back into the crook of his arm and started forward again.

For the first time since she'd left him in Colorado, she

was where she needed to be. The restlessness, the emptiness, the despair—all of it was gone, and she felt as if she could breathe again.

For a long minute, the only sounds were the steady rhythm of the waves slapping the shore and the distant strains of the live music coming from the thatched bar where Reed and his guests were hanging out.

"I'm sorry." The words finally fell out.

He glanced at her sideways but didn't say anything, clearly giving her the space to say what she needed without pushing her. Just one more thing she loved about him.

She inhaled, knowing she had to keep going. He'd already proven that he cared. Now it was her turn to do the same. "I shouldn't have run off the way I did after you told me you loved me."

His steps slowed, and his body tensed beneath her fingertips.

"It was rude of me to leave without even saying goodbye."

"I understand." His voice was soft. "I pushed too hard—"

"No. You didn't." She stopped walking and turned to face him. "None of it was you. It was all me."

In the glow of the evening, his features looked darker and more rugged, but his expression was as tender as always.

"Can you forgive me?"

"Oh, darlin', there's nothing to forgive—"

"Yes, there is. Please accept my apology for running away and not answering your texts and calls and being so stubborn."

"All right."

"You forgive me?"

"Yep."

"As easy as that?"

"Easy as that."

She should have known that Brock would forgive as easily as he loved. That was just the way he was. But he deserved more of an explanation, and she wanted to give it to him. "I was scared—have been scared for a long time. And I think I was using Reed as an excuse to keep me safe from the heartache I've seen my mom go through."

He nodded, his gaze languidly taking in her face as though he couldn't get enough of her—at least, she hoped that was what his gazing meant.

"Maybe I've been trying to protect myself. But I've realized that self-protection is really just hurting me."

"We're all running from demons of some kind from our pasts."

Her heart swelled with more love for this man, for how understanding he was, how kind, how caring. Even if the thought of being in a permanent relationship was still daunting, she wanted to be with Brock, wanted to try it.

She blew out a breath and made herself say the truth. "I realized that I don't love Reed…"

His eyes snapped to hers and rounded with surprise. "You don't?"

"Not the way I love you."

He grew absolutely motionless, wasn't even breathing.

"I love you, Brock." She wanted to reach for his hands, clasp them in hers, but she still had no right to assume he would try their relationship again, this time for real. "I know I don't deserve you, not after the way I shut you out. But if you're still open to seeing where our relationship could go, I'd like another chance."

He lifted a hand to her face and caressed her cheek. "If you really want to be with me, I'm warning you that it's gonna be real hard—"

"I realize all relationships face challenges—"

He touched her lips and silenced her. "It's gonna be real hard because I'll probably drive you crazy with how crazy I am about you."

All the tension that had been building over the past two weeks slid away, and happiness rolled in to replace it. She couldn't hold back a smile. "I think I can handle your craziness."

"Do you?" His grin kicked up again.

"I might even like that craziness."

He let her sandals fall from his grip, set his hands on

her hips, and drew her closer. "Good. Because I'm totally and completely and madly in love with you in a way I've never been with anyone else and never will be with any other woman."

The sincerity and softness of his declaration ricocheted through her body. "Really?"

He nodded and bent his head toward hers.

She caught the scent of his woodsy aftershave, and desire curled through her.

"I'll give you all the time you need to figure out where you want our relationship to go and to be ready for more. But I already know what I want."

"You do?"

"Yep. I want you. That's all. As long as I have you, I'll be a happy man."

He brushed his nose against hers, and she closed her eyes as contentment welled up from deep inside. This was right where she wanted to be, and he was all she wanted too.

Well, maybe she wanted more...like to kiss him again, and this time to never have to stop.

She dropped her clutch and wrap to the ground, then leaned into him and fused her mouth with his. And oh, oh, oh. The taste of him, the feel of him, the warmth of him—he was heavenly. With his lips molding to hers, she nearly groaned with need.

She wound her arms behind his head and lifted into

him, taking the kiss deeper and moving into it more fully. The pressure and the rhythm of their lips together picked up immediately, turning hungry and urgent, as if they were making up for the past two weeks of being apart.

Maybe they were making up for lost time, but there was also no denying that the chemistry between them was strong. It had been smoldering all along, sizzling into sparks whenever they touched. It was sizzling now too, sending heat to her limbs and fingers and toes.

She had the feeling that kissing him would be one of her favorite things to do, which was saying something, because doing everything with him so far had been fun. But this kissing? It was incredible. Because he was incredible.

His hands glided up her hips to her back. His hold was hard and firm, but also possessive. As he slid one of his hands higher to her bare back where her sundress dipped down, his thumb reverently caressed her skin.

She couldn't hold back a soft moan of pleasure.

He in turn gave a throaty response before deepening the kiss so that suddenly, she felt in a free fall with him, spinning wildly. He was exciting, and their relationship would be thrilling and passionate and full of life. She had no doubt about that.

But could she love him in return the way he deserved?

The question broke through all her emotion, and she pulled back from him abruptly and took a step away.

Her chest rose and fell heavily as she struggled to find a breath and her equilibrium.

He was breathing heavily too. But a lazy smile was working up one corner of his mouth, making him look irresistibly handsome—so much so that she wanted to throw herself against him and drag his head down to hers again to fuse their mouths into one.

All she knew was that Brock McQuaid was one of a kind, and she wanted to be worthy of a man like him. She wanted to love him as well as he loved her—wanted to treat him special, wanted to sacrifice for him, wanted to forgive him easily, wanted to persevere with him, and wanted to make him happy. But could she really do all of that?

She crossed her arms over her chest to hold back a shiver. "I'm afraid, Brock."

22

"Afraid?" Brock wanted to reach for Venus and draw her back, but instead, he stuffed his hands into his pockets. "What are you afraid of, darlin'?"

She rubbed her arms and stared out over the ocean. With the breeze molding her sundress to her figure, she was picture-perfect, especially with her cheeks flushed and her lips swollen from their kissing.

His entire chest was burning for her. He hadn't expected a reunion to happen, hadn't even in his wildest dreams believed Venus would approach him today and declare her love.

He could still hardly believe it, and a part of him was waiting to wake up and find out this wasn't real. Maybe he'd even already spooked her with how passionately he'd kissed her. He had to remember not to overwhelm her with his feelings, because now that he'd seen her again, his passion for her was stronger than ever.

"Don't hold back on me." He kept his voice soft. "Let's promise each other we'll talk about everything we're feeling."

She nodded, then tore her gaze away from the ocean and settled her beautiful blue eyes back on him. "You're so good at loving me and had such a good model from your father. But I'm afraid I won't be able to love you as well."

The unanswered text from his dad burned in his pocket. Maybe he hadn't always seen eye to eye with his dad, but through it all, his dad had continued to be there for him. And Venus was right. His dad had been a good model in how to live and love.

It was past time to text his dad back and thank him for his encouragement with Venus.

"What if I fail?" Venus's voice was low and filled with doubts. "I didn't have the same kind of example that you did. In fact, my mom's relationships always fail."

"Even with my good example, I've done a lot wrong. The key is that we have to make our own choices on how we want to love."

She nodded slowly.

"No matter our pasts, we get to write the story we want for our future."

"I like that."

"Besides, you've got one important thing that your mom doesn't have." He grinned. "Me. I've got enough love for the both of us, and it'll see us through whatever comes our way."

"That's not fair to make you take on that responsibility."

"I can't help it. It's just the way it is."

His head was spinning with all the lyrics that had started formulating again almost the second he'd laid eyes on her. He had the feeling that from here on out, all his songs would be about her. And that was perfectly fine with him.

"Hey!" came a shout from the beach, down by the thatched bar.

They turned to find that Reed had stepped outside the bar area. "You coming? We're getting ready to sit down for dinner."

Brock wasn't all that keen on being around Reed, not after the cold welcome earlier. But if Reed was important to Venus, then he'd do everything he could to get along with the guy. "What do you say? Should we go join the party?"

She hesitated. Then she nodded. "As much as I'd like to have you all to myself, I suppose this weekend is about Reed and not about us."

Brock held out his hand to Venus this time. No more holding elbows. As she slipped her hand into his, he laced their fingers together, loving her silky skin and her pretty nails and her graceful wrists with simple gold bracelets.

He gathered up her sandals, purse, and shawl, and held them as they walked back. He wanted to say more to her, wanted to tell her he loved her again, wanted to stop and kiss her one more time.

But Reed's narrowed gaze was upon them, watching carefully as if he were Venus's guardian and didn't approve of them being together.

As they drew nearer, the lively music wafted toward them as did the conversations coming from the bar that opened up to the infinity pool. Reed's friends were still standing around the bar sipping drinks and hadn't been seated yet.

Was it time for dinner? Or had Reed just wanted to put an end to Brock's time alone with Venus?

"What's this?" Reed looked pointedly at their joined hands. "Have you decided to keep your fake relationship going after all?"

His question was loud enough to carry, and the chatter of the others in the bar began to fade. Didn't he care who heard their conversation?

Venus stiffened. "Reed, don't do this."

"Do what?" Reed's voice rose a notch. "Talk about the fact that your managers set you up in a relationship to help your images?"

While the band was still playing, the laughter and voices had quieted, and all eyes were upon the three of them, especially upon Venus. A visitor in a far corner had raised his camera and was likely getting the interaction on video.

Why was Reed doing this? He had to realize that revealing the details of the fake relationship would be damaging to Venus. If he was really a good friend, then why wasn't he being more careful?

Brock wanted to walk over and punch Reed in the face for being so insensitive to Venus, but he didn't want that to show up on someone's social media in five minutes.

"Reed, please." Venus's features creased with distress. "Can we talk privately?"

Reed waved his hand around the bar. "Why don't you tell everyone how even the *Rolling Stone* article was fake?"

Venus seemed to shrink back at all the faces staring at her.

Frustration only reared up all the more inside Brock. Over the years, Reed had been a good friend to Venus. Brock had never doubted that. Was Reed jealous that Venus was finally finding happiness of her own? Maybe he'd wanted Lexi but also expected Venus to always be there for him too.

Whatever the case, Brock couldn't stand back and watch him tear apart Venus. He started to release Venus's hand and take a step toward Reed, but Venus clung to him, sliding both arms around Brock and hugging him from the side.

"There's nothing fake about my relationship with Brock McQuaid." Her voice rang out over the music. "In fact, there's nothing more real on this earth than my love for this man. My love for him is the most real thing I've ever felt."

As she said the words, she looked up at Brock, her eyes brimming with a love that sent a tremor through him.

He couldn't keep himself from dipping down and stealing a kiss from her. It was quick, but it was hard and hot.

She braced a hand against his chest and dug her fingers into his shirt, then smiled up at him. "All I know is that Brock McQuaid's love for me has made me a better woman, and I plan to spend the rest of my life showing him how much I love him in return."

This time she reached up, wrapped both arms around his neck, and kissed him with a passion that was strong and fierce and determined and communicated all her love. He could feel it in every move, so much so that his chest ached from the relief of knowing that she wanted him and that everything she was feeling was genuine.

As they kissed, the crowd began to clap. Within seconds, everyone was stomping and whistling and cheering their approval. Everyone except Reed, who had lowered himself into the nearest chair and hung his head.

Venus broke away, a beautiful smile lighting up her

face and her eyes. She peered up at Brock and cupped his cheek. "If you're still planning to leave Los Cabos, I'd love to catch a ride with you."

"I'm leaving." He said so because he could tell that was what she wanted, that she needed to take a break from Reed. Whatever their friendship had once been, it could no longer be the same. Maybe it would just take time for Reed to figure that out. At least, Brock hoped so.

"Then let's go." She grabbed Brock's hand and began to lead him through the bar and away from the others.

When they stepped outside onto the short pathway that led to the lobby, Brock bent and placed a kiss on her head. "I'm proud of you, darlin'. That wasn't easy."

She nodded, her smile fading. "Reed's mad at me now."

Brock wanted to say that Reed was a scumbag for hurting Venus the way he had. But Venus needed his reassurance, not his anger. "He won't want to lose you as a friend, so he'll come around eventually."

"I hope so."

Brock wrapped his arm around her waist, reveling in the fact that he could do so now. She'd said she wanted to spend the rest of her life loving him. Maybe not in those exact words, but she'd all but told him and the world that she wanted to marry him.

He had half a mind to drop to his knees right here in the middle of the pathway and propose to her. But when he proposed—and he would—he planned to make it special. As his dad said, he had to go big or go home.

She leaned her head against his arm. "I guess everyone will find out about our fake relationship agreement now."

"It doesn't matter."

"But the gossip will ruin your image again. After you've worked so hard to repair it, I don't want that to happen."

Brock stopped her and let himself caress her cheek again, something he could do every day and never get tired of. "Listen, darlin', someone really smart once told me the negativity doesn't last long and that my charm comes through for me."

"Someone really smart did tell you that, didn't she?"

"Yep."

She hesitated. "Still, if people realize we had an arrangement to fake date, it'll be really bad for you."

He just shrugged. "All that matters is you. If you're happy, then I'll be happy."

She watched him for a long moment, her eyes wide and filling with wonder. "I'm so lucky to have you, you know that?"

"Nope, I'm the lucky one."

She brushed a finger over his cheek, the same way he'd just done to her. "I have an idea for how to make any new rumors about us being in a fake relationship go away."

"Oh yeah? What?"

"Everywhere we go, we can prove we're in love."

He liked that idea. A lot. "How we gonna do that?" He couldn't keep his voice from growing husky with desire.

Her lashes fell halfway, and she wrapped her hand behind his neck, gliding her fingers into his hair. "I'll show you how."

And she did. She captured his mouth in a kiss that left no doubt that they were in love.

23

Venus stood on the side stage of Brock's concert, his first of the new year, the first after the past months of recording his newest album.

As the strains of his song came to an end, she joined the crowd in clapping for him. The latest songs were his best. One of them was at the top of the Country Music Charts and had been since he'd released the single a few months ago. Two other songs on the album were also in the top twenty. With the album's full release today, his manager and label had alerted him that he was having his highest sales to date.

Brock swiped off his cowboy hat, lifted it in the air, and gave the crowd his trademark grin. It was the one that had made every woman fall in love with him since he'd first stepped onto the stage years ago and still made women scream for him everywhere he went...even though Venus had tried to make it very clear over recent months that Brock was hers and hers alone.

Thankfully, Reed's public announcements about her and Brock at his bachelor party hadn't amounted to more than a small blip in the gossip and news. The video that had been posted of Reed accusing her of staging a relationship with Brock had made the rounds on social media for a day or two. But then they'd been overshadowed by all the other pictures fans had started taking of her and Brock together—a lot of them kissing, touching each other's faces, holding hands, and some of them laughing and smiling together or just talking.

Brock had relished their efforts to prove their love, so much so that she'd had fun with it too. She'd put forth her best effort to show the world how much she adored Brock McQuaid. She'd enjoyed showering Brock with affection everywhere they went. And he'd loved every minute of her attention, soaking it in as if she and her touches were the sustenance of his life.

Now, it seemed natural to always be touching or kissing or holding him. The world had accepted them as a couple, and everyone else had too, including Reed.

He'd called her and apologized the next morning, claimed he'd been tipsy when he'd blurted out the confidential information about her relationship with Brock. He'd also admitted he'd been jealous that Brock was still so important to her. When she'd asked Reed why he was opposed to Brock, he hadn't been able to answer, hadn't been able to list any concerns other than what he'd already said.

When he'd asked her to come back for the remainder of the weekend, she'd told him she needed time to sort through all that had happened and that he did too.

She almost hadn't attended his wedding because he'd still been upset with her. But in the end, she and Brock had gone as guests, stayed for the ceremony and not the reception, and then left.

Eventually, she and Reed had had more conversations. They'd confessed that once upon a time they'd harbored deeper feelings for each other, but for whatever reason, neither of them had been able to vocalize or act on those feelings. They'd agreed that things had worked out the way they were supposed to, and they'd each be happier with someone else.

Their relationship hadn't been the same since Los Cabos, but she'd accepted that it would have to change now that he was married and she was in a serious relationship. The truth was, she was okay with the change and didn't need Reed the same way anymore, because Brock was not only the man she loved but also her best friend.

And oh, she loved him.

As he set his hat back on his head, her heart squeezed hard at the sight of him in all his rugged charm on stage in front of the roaring crowd. He deserved the praise for such beautiful and heartfelt songs.

Songs she'd inspired.

She smiled. Brock gave her all the credit for his songs and music, said she was the inspiration behind everything he thought of and wrote. But she also had seen firsthand just how much work went into producing the songs and then recording them. Brock had labored tirelessly over the fall, mostly from his ranch outside of Nashville, where he could be close to his label and the studio there.

She'd had a busy fall too, traveling around the world as usual for more events and photo shoots than she'd ever had before. She and Brock had spent as much time together as possible, meeting for long weekends or even for a day here and there. They'd gone back to the Colorado ranch a couple of times and visited his family. But the time with him was never enough, and she had begun to dread her trips and was tired of the traveling.

So a few weeks ago, she'd had a meeting with her agent and her agency and had come up with a new plan. She'd just gotten word today, before flying to Atlanta for Brock's concert, that her plan had been approved—a plan to open her own clothing and makeup lines, which would allow her to travel less and focus more on her new business.

She hadn't told Brock about it yet and was waiting to do so until they were alone later tonight, maybe on one of their all-night dates that they still loved to do.

"Thank you, Atlanta!" Brock called again.

The crowd was still cheering, and Brock glanced at her on the side stage, then winked.

Her heart melted, and she couldn't keep from thinking about the first concert of his she'd gone to in Berlin and how he'd winked at her then too.

"You want another song?" Brock asked the crowd.

The roars in response were deafening.

Brock nodded at his band, clearly having an encore ready. "This is a new song I wrote," he said above the noise. "And nope, it's not on my new album."

That announcement brought more cheers.

He strummed his guitar, situating it in his arms. "Actually this is a very special song for a very special woman in my life."

A special song? What was that about? Most of the time, Brock shared his new songs with her first, even before his band and his producer.

Venus could hear the shouts of her name coming from different places in the stadium. Everyone knew who the special woman in his life was, and she loved that they'd accepted her as his girlfriend and seemed to love her too.

As Brock's bandmates joined in the melody, he strummed for a few more chords before leaning into the mic and singing the first line of the song.

"You were climbing up to heaven back where
    you belong
But you slipped and fell, lucky for me I was
    coming along
When I caught you I knew I had an angel in
    my hands
One sent straight from God to make me a
    better man."

The melody was so exquisitely beautiful and the strains so poignant that her heart tugged with longing—longing for Brock, for their love, for their life together.

"You deserve heaven, but all I have is earth,
I'll spend eternity givin' you everything you're worth
Darlin', you're my angel, you're my life
So just tell me yes, you'll be my wife."

Venus's breath caught. He wasn't really asking her to be his wife, was he? He was just singing a song. And those were the lyrics.

He glanced her way, and something in his expression brought her racing thoughts to a halt. As he started the next stanza of the ballad, about how he'd stayed out all night, how the moonlight had created a halo over her head, and then how she'd become his inspiration, tears were pricking her eyes.

He was definitely singing about her.

While his songs had been inspired by their love, none had ever been quite so specific about their relationship. When he began the bridge and ended with the chorus, this time he stopped playing his guitar, set it aside, and lowered himself to one knee, facing her.

As he sang the words "So just tell me yes, you'll be my wife," he held out a small ring box and flipped it open.

Was this really happening? Here? Now? Was he proposing to her?

They'd talked about marriage on several occasions over the past months of officially dating. The last conversation had been in Paris at the top of the Eiffel Tower a few weeks ago when he'd flown over to visit her for a weekend. She'd told him she was ready to marry him and choose to commit to him forever. Yes, choose. She knew she might always have some baggage from her past, but she wanted to push past it and make a life with Brock.

Clearly, Brock had taken their conversation to heart.

The crowd was going wild again.

She could only press her hands to her heart and stare at Brock.

He grinned at her and waited.

Ella Mae, who'd been standing close and was now beaming, gave Venus a nudge. "Well, go on out there."

Venus had dressed casually for the concert, just a pair

of ripped Levi's and a bulky cream sweater along with the cute cowboy boots Brock had bought for her during one of her trips to Nashville. She wasn't wearing an elegant gown, and this wasn't an elegant party. It was better. It was from Brock's heart and full of his love. And she couldn't ask for anything more.

With a thrill building inside her, she crossed out of the darkness of the side stage, her gaze never once leaving Brock's. As she stepped onto the main stage and began to make her way to Brock, the crowd was again deafening, nearly delirious with their happiness at being present to witness Brock McQuaid proposing.

She stopped in front of him, still clutching her heart.

From his spot on one knee, he peered up at her with his gentle brown eyes. "Darlin', I love you. Will you make me the happiest man alive by agreeing to marry me?"

She could hardly hear Brock over the cheering, but she heard enough.

"Yes!" she shouted while holding out her hand. "I'll be your wife!"

As she repeated the lyrics to his newest song, his grin turned up even higher into that million-dollar hunk smile that always made her stomach flip.

In the next instant, he was slipping a ring on her finger, an elegant oval diamond that was tasteful and perfect and just her style. She held it out and examined it on her finger. Brock was back on his feet and pulling her into his arms.

She went to him willingly and hugged him with all the love that she'd never known she could feel for one man.

Author's Note

Hi friends! I hope you enjoyed this second book in my new contemporary romance series! I had a lot of fun writing Brock and Venus's love story, and I hope you had just as much fun reading it.

I admit, while growing up I was never a huge fan of country music. But over recent years, after my kids began listening to it, I've heard more (sometimes lots more!) and have been surprised at the catchy tunes as well as the solid messages in some of the songs. I'm not sure if I'm a die-hard fan of country music yet, but it's slowly growing on me, especially after researching and writing this book.

You might be wondering which McQuaid sibling's story is coming after this (at least, I hope you're excited to keep reading about this lovable family!). Drumroll, please! The only girl of the family, Emberly, is getting her love story next. If you like the secret prince trope, then you won't want to miss her story!

As always, I love hearing from YOU! If you haven't

yet joined my Facebook Reader Room, what are you waiting for!? It's a great place to keep up to date on all my book releases and book news as well as a fun place to connect with other readers and me.

Until next time…

P.S. In case you missed **Spurs and Sparks**, the first book in the Healing Springs Ranch series, read on for a small taste of Tyler and Kinsey's story!

SPURS and SPARKS

JODY HEDLUND

A HEALING SPRINGS RANCH NOVEL

SPURS *and* SPARKS

JODY HEDLUND

NORTHERN LIGHTS PRESS

"Dad, why don't you have yourself a woman?"

Tyler McQuaid, in the middle of casting his fishing line, slipped on the wet stones beneath his waders. He threw out both hands and tried to steady himself, but the rushing river was too strong. In the next instant, he found himself falling backward into the mountain runoff, still icy cold for May. He landed with a splash, his fly rod falling from his grip into the Badger River.

A dozen paces ahead in the shallow water, Wyatt glanced over his shoulder, his innocent seven-year-old eyes widening. "What's wrong?"

Sitting waist-deep in the river, Tyler could only stare at his son, a miniature version of himself with a stocky frame, dark-brown hair, deep-set eyes, and a strong, square jawline. The kid was wearing a black Stetson and was outfitted in his own waders and flannel shirt, just like Tyler's.

"Dad?" Wyatt persisted as he swiped up the pole floating past him.

"Your question surprised me a little. That's all."

Perched on a log a short distance from the river, Anson guffawed obnoxiously. The old cowboy-turned-nanny paused in his whittling of mushroom replicas to lift his brows at Tyler, his eyes saying everything—that Wyatt's question hadn't surprised him just *a little*. No, it had surprised him so much that it had knocked him off his feet.

Anson's long gray hair was slicked back and covered with a battered and sweat-stained cowboy hat that was probably as old as the cowboy himself. He was wiry and short and muscular, still fit from his days as a horse jockey.

As Tyler began to push up from the river, he glared at the man. "I don't need any of your smart-aleck remarks tonight."

Anson's gap-toothed smile wrinkled his leathery face. "I didn't say anything."

"I asked the question, Dad." Wyatt started wading upriver, his own child-sized fly-fishing pole in one hand and Tyler's much longer rod in the other.

The slant of the sun coming off the western mountain range turned the water droplets into diamonds. The sunlight also glinted on the fir trees mingling with the aspens that were bright with new leaves and rustling in the mountain breeze. It was the most peaceful and most beautiful time of the day in the high country of Colorado.

Tyler sighed. Too bad they couldn't ever just fish in silence.

But no. Wyatt usually had something to say. "At school today, Levi wanted to know why you don't have a woman."

"Why are you guys talking about a subject like that?" Water droplets rolled down Tyler's water-resistant pants and boots, although he already could feel the chill and dampness of the water against his skin.

"He heard his mom talking about you and saying it was past time for you to have a woman."

Tyler frowned. Nettie needed to be more careful what she was talking about around her son. Neither Levi nor Wyatt was old enough to understand anything about relationships, particularly about divorce. Wyatt had been only two when Stephanie left. He'd never known what it was like to have a mother around.

So why the curiosity now?

"Thirty-two's not all that old."

"It's ancient, Dad."

Anson chortled outright, the cackling rising above the rustling river and echoing in the stillness of the evening.

Tyler glared again at the cowboy nanny who'd been working for the family since Tyler was a boy. "I'm not as ancient as Anson."

"Anson says he has all kinds of women."

"Oh really?" Tyler cocked a brow at the old man.

Anson bent his head and studied his mushroom intently, smoothing away shavings and rubbing at it as if it were the most important thing in the world.

"Oh, that's right." Tyler didn't let up. "Anson has all those girlfriends at his Saturday night senior bingo club."

Anson spit on his thumb and then wiped a spot on the mushroom. "At least I got some pretty ladies who like me. That's more than I can say for you."

"I think Levi's mom likes Dad." Wyatt just shrugged. "At least, that's what Levi said."

Tyler shook his head as he neared Wyatt. "We're doing all right without a woman, aren't we?"

Wyatt handed him the wayward pole, his expression serious. "Why don't you want a woman? It might be real nice to have one around."

"We have Grandma and Aunt Emberly."

This time Anson snorted, and it was loud enough to rival a moose about to charge.

"Besides," Tyler continued without giving Wyatt a chance to say that Grandma and Aunt Emberly didn't count. "I'm busy with the ranch. You know that."

He'd taken over managing their luxury ranch resort from his dad the year he'd graduated from the University of Colorado, and he'd been in charge ever since. Ten years, to be exact.

Of course, his dad had continued to help in a public-relations role, which suited his personality better than the everyday management of the ranch's operations.

"You've got the ranch running great." Wyatt spoke with a seriousness that a child of seven shouldn't have. "Maybe you should focus on something else now. Like getting me a mom."

Tyler opened his mouth to respond, but nothing came out. What could he say anyway? Wyatt already had a mom, but maybe the boy wasn't satisfied with the once- or twice-a-year visits with Stephanie and was beginning to want more than just a dad provided.

"Listen, Wyatt—" At the buzz of his phone, he fished it out of his back pocket to see his mom's name and profile filling the screen. He tapped open the call. "Hi, Mom."

"Tyler." His mom's voice was breathless and strained.

"What's up?" With the dry fly missing from his line, Tyler began to slosh toward his tacklebox sitting on the river's edge near Anson.

"It's your dad."

Stepping out onto the rocky embankment, Tyler came to an immediate halt.

"He's having back pain again," his mom rushed. "It's so bad that he fell and can't get up."

Dad had been having bouts of back pain recently, and Tyler had tried to make him take it easy. Of course, Dad was a stubborn and determined McQuaid and never rested.

"Where are you?"

"We're at the house."

"Don't try to lift him. I'll be right there."

"He's throwing up, Ty." Mom's voice wavered with worry. "And he's complaining of stomach pain now too."

"This sounds more serious than just a strained back."

"I think so too."

Tyler's mind whirred. He had to come up with a solution and manage the situation. Fast. "We need to take him in to the ER."

"That's what I was thinking. I've already asked Kade to get the helicopter ready."

In Park County, the ranch wasn't near an emergency room. For severe situations, they almost always used the helicopter and flew to Colorado Springs, which was only about sixty miles away. His youngest brother, Kade, had a pilot's license and was the one they relied on to get them where they needed to go.

"I'm worried, Ty," his mom whispered, probably trying to keep Dad from hearing her.

"It'll be fine." At least, Tyler hoped it would be. "Hold tight, and I'll be there in a few minutes."

He ended the call and then shot a quick call to Kade. As he finished and stuffed his phone into his pocket, Anson was at his side, his forehead furrowed.

"Something wrong with T.W.?"

"More back pain." All the employees at Healing Springs Ranch loved his dad, especially the old-timers like Anson.

Anson's scowl deepened. Since he lived at the main house, he'd heard Dad's recent complaints about his back. Just yesterday, Dad had tried to put on his cowboy boots and had nearly buckled over with a spasm.

They should have taken Dad to the doctor then. When they'd suggested it, Dad had claimed he was okay.

They'd believed him. Because Dad had always been as healthy as a horse—active and alert, energetic and enthusiastic, calling Tyler with new ideas and plans, his vision for the ranch still alive and abounding, even though he'd pulled back to give Tyler the final say on everything.

"C'mon, Wyatt. Time to go." He regretted that he had to cut short their Friday activity night, but there wasn't even time to gather up their fly-fishing gear. He'd send one of the employees out to retrieve everything later. For now, he needed to get to Dad and figure out what was going on.

Tyler climbed to the UTV on the trail above the river. He slid into the driver's seat and started up the vehicle. A moment later, Wyatt and Anson were scrambling into the back seats. Tyler waited for them to buckle in, then he gunned the small four-wheeled off-road vehicle down the trail.

He wound his way along the paths behind the largest and most elaborate of the private luxury cabins. All of them were styled in Western themes and furnished with only the best furniture and appliances. They had full-sized kitchens, king suites, spacious lofts, sitting areas with wood-burning fireplaces, private patios with hot tubs, and more.

The smaller cabins were no less lavish and were beautifully decorated with screened-in porches that faced the river. Although equipped with kitchenettes, most of the guests took their meals in the Cliffside Dining Room in the lodge, where the chef prepared daily farm-to-table meals that everyone raved about. The ranch also had a smaller dining area in Brook Barn that offered simpler fare and snacks.

As Tyler reached the main pathway, he jerked to a stop while a young couple meandered past, walking hand in hand, likely staying in one of their honeymoon cabins, which were a Forbes Travel Guide five-star recommendation.

As soon as he started forward, he veered onto the uphill lane that led to his family's home. The main house was set away from the resort to allow for privacy but was still close enough that they could be involved in any issues and needs that might arise.

At the sound of the chopper engine and wings roaring to life at the landing pad on a plateau above the house,

Tyler released a pent-up breath. Kade was ready to go, probably already had the stretcher at the house.

As Tyler flew up the final incline, the modern two-story log home came into view on the rise. With a prominent peaked prow at the center and windows from floor to ceiling, the great room faced the west so that viewing sunsets was almost a nightly occasion.

On each side of the peak, the house sprawled out with additional tall windows. A large deck on the main level of the house contained a hot tub and patio furniture, while a porch swing and hammock were positioned on the grassy knoll underneath.

Tyler steered the UTV around the driveway that led to the back of the house, which had a cozy but small porch with rustic-looking rocking chairs. The ranch's interior decorator had styled their home both inside and out with Western-themed decorations like all the other homes on the ranch, and it was just as interesting and unique.

The main house had six bedrooms, which was plenty big enough for him and each of his four siblings to have had their own rooms while growing up. Now only he and Wyatt lived there with Mom and Dad.

As head wrangler, Kade preferred bunking with the other ranch hands in one of the apartments over the main barn. His sister Emberly, who was the events manager, stayed in one of the employee cottages near the main lodge. Of course, Brock was busy with his career as a country music singer, and ever since Dustin had left his position as an elite army ranger, he'd put his skills to use as a bodyguard for an executive protection company and traveled all over the world for his work.

Yes indeed, he and Wyatt and Mom and Dad had more than enough space. Sometimes too much.

Tyler halted the UTV and jumped out. He didn't wait for Wyatt or Anson—was grateful in this instant to know that Anson was taking care of the boy. Instead, Tyler bolted into the house and to his parents' bedroom.

"Hey," he called, stepping into the spacious room.

Mom stepped out of the master bathroom, tears streaking her face.

With her wavy red hair pulled back into a clip, she appeared younger than her fifty-five years and was still as beautiful as in the pictures on the wall from when she'd been crowned Miss Colorado years earlier.

"How is he?"

"Oh Tyler, I'm so worried. He's in terrible pain and can't stop moaning."

Tyler sidled past her into the bathroom with its clean white interior, jacuzzi tub, and walk-in shower. It was more spacious than most bathrooms, with two walk-in closets, a dressing table, and a chaise. He halted at the sight of his brawny dad writhing on the ground, clutching his stomach and moaning.

Tyler's chest tightening, he dropped to his knees beside the man who had been not only his mentor and friend but also the rock who'd held him up through some really hard years.

"Dad." Tyler touched his dad's arm gently.

The moaning halted, and his dad's eyes flew open. The dark brown, usually so honest and kind, was now filled with fear. He reached out a hand and grasped Tyler's. "Son, I'm dying."

GET YOUR COPY OF *SPURS AND SPARKS* NOW!!

Find out where the McQuaid family began in the Colorado Cowboys series, a heart-warming, historical romance series. Join the McQuaid family as they seek new opportunities and find love in the wild and unsettled land of Colorado in the 1860s.

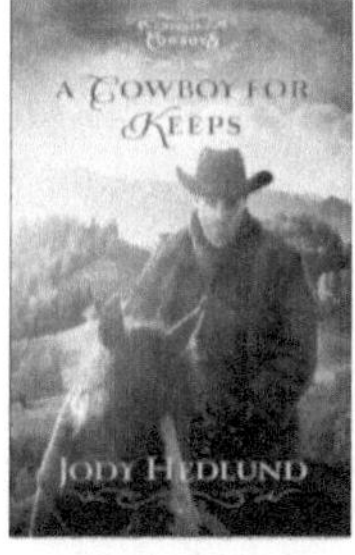

A Cowboy for Keeps

Wyatt McQuaid is struggling to get his new ranch up and running and is in town to purchase cattle when the mayor proposes the most unlikely of bargains. He'll invest in a herd of cattle for Wyatt's ranch if Wyatt agrees to help the town become more respectable by marrying and starting a family. And the mayor has just the candidate in mind for Wyatt to marry.

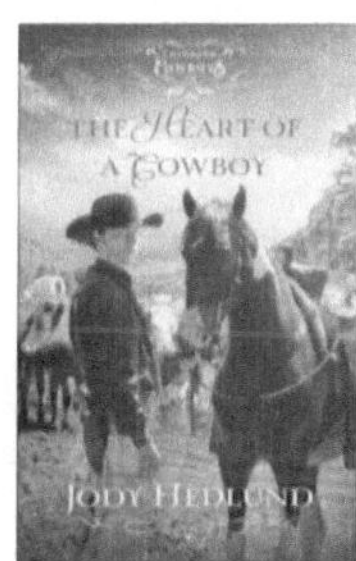

The Heart of a Cowboy

After watching his ma suffer and die in childbirth, Flynn McQuaid has sworn off women and marriage forever. Headed west to start a new life, he has his hands full not only taking care of his younger siblings but also delivering cattle to his older brother. He doesn't need more complications in falling for a woman he's determined not to love.

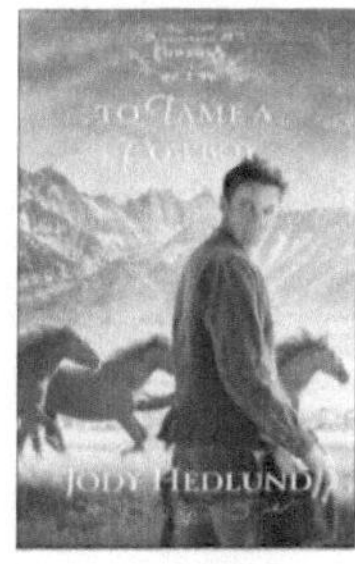

To Tame a Cowboy

Brody McQuaid is a broken man, and he knows it. While his body survived the war, his soul did not. Besides loving his little niece, his only sense of purpose comes from saving the wild horses that roam South Park. When the new veterinarian on the ranch turns her gentle healing touch on him, he's not sure that he's ready to tame his fears.

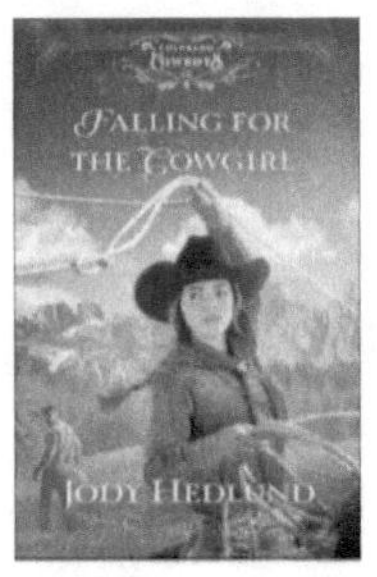

Falling for the Cowgirl

As the only girl in her family, and with four older brothers, Ivy McQuaid can rope and ride with the roughest of ranchers. She's ready to have what she's always longed for—a home of her own. She's set her heart on a parcel of land south of Fairplay and is saving for it with her winnings from the cowhand competitions she sneaks into. But her dream is put in jeopardy when the man she once loved reappears in her life.

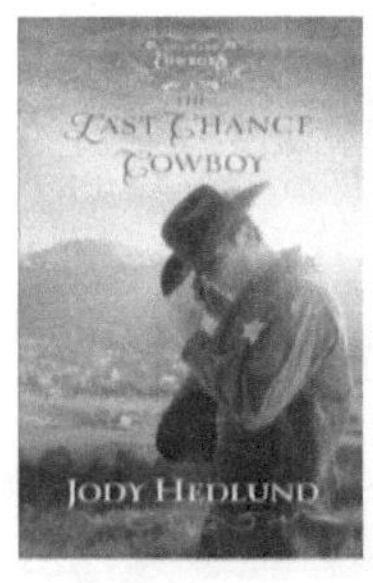

Last Chance Cowboy

The repentant prodigal Dylan McQuaid is finally back in Fairplay. As sheriff, he's doing his best to prove to the town he's a changed man and worthy of their trust. When a woman shows up with an infant son he didn't know he had, Dylan is left with only complicated choices on what to do next.

Jody Hedlund is the bestselling author of more than sixty novels and is the winner of numerous awards. Jody lives in Michigan with her husband, busy family, and five spoiled cats. She writes sweet romances with plenty of sizzle.

A complete list of my novels can be found at jody hedlund.com.

Would you like to know when my next book is available? You can sign up for my newsletter, become my friend on Goodreads, like me on Facebook, or follow me on Instagram.

Newsletter: jodyhedlund.com
Facebook: AuthorJodyHedlund
Instagram: @JodyHedlund

9 7 9 8 9 8 9 6 2 7 7 6 9